Images of Olivia flashed through Craig's head

Then another image appeared—the attacker waiting for her when she'd arrived home, ambushing her. The Savannah Squares and graveyard whirled past. Concrete tombstones and monuments stood in rows, the symbols of death macabre in the murky gray light. The fear that Olivia might be severely injured twisted his insides.

He'd told her he'd take care of things—had promised to protect her....

But he'd failed and now someone had tried to kill her.

It seemed like an eternity, but he finally reached the street to her apartment. As soon as he reached the porch stoop, he saw her lying on the ground near the flower bed.

"Olivia, can you hear me?" Craig's throat jammed as he knelt and checked her pulse. It was weak and thready, but she was alive....

Dear Harlequin Intrigue Reader,

Summer's winding down, but Harlequin Intrigue is as hot as ever with six spine-tingling reads for you this month!

* Our new BIG SKY BOUNTY HUNTERS promotion debuts with Amanda Stevens's *Going to Extremes*. In the coming months, look for more titles from Jessica Andersen, Cassie Miles and Julie Miller.

* We have some great miniseries for you. Rita Herron is back with *Mysterious Circumstances*, the latest in her NIGHTHAWK ISLAND series. Mallory Kane's *Seeking Asylum* is the third book in her ULTIMATE AGENTS series. And Sylvie Kurtz has another tale in THE SEEKERS series—*Eye of a Hunter*.

* No month would be complete without a chilling gothic romance. This month's ECLIPSE title is Debra Webb's *Urban Sensation*.

* Jan Hambright, a fabulous new author, makes her debut with *Relentless*. Sparks fly when a feisty repo agent repossesses a BMW with an ex-homicide detective in the trunk!

Don't miss a single book this month and every month!

Sincerely,

Denise O'Sullivan
Senior Editor
Harlequin Intrigue

MYSTERIOUS CIRCUMSTANCES

RITA HERRON

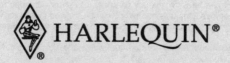

TORONTO • NEW YORK • LONDON
AMSTERDAM • PARIS • SYDNEY • HAMBURG
STOCKHOLM • ATHENS • TOKYO • MILAN • MADRID
PRAGUE • WARSAW • BUDAPEST • AUCKLAND

ISBN 0-373-22861-9

MYSTERIOUS CIRCUMSTANCES

This edition published by arrangement with Harlequin Books S.A.

® and TM are trademarks of the publisher. Trademarks indicated with ® are registered in the United States Patent and Trademark Office, the Canadian Trade Marks Office and in other countries.

www.eHarlequin.com

Printed in U.S.A.

ABOUT THE AUTHOR

Award-winning author Rita Herron wrote her first book when she was twelve, but didn't think real people grew up to be writers. Now she writes so she doesn't have to get a *real* job. A former kindergarten teacher and workshop leader, she traded her storytelling for kids for romance, and writes romantic comedies and romantic suspense. She lives in Georgia with her own romance hero and three kids. She loves to hear from readers, so please write her at P.O. Box 921225, Norcross, GA 30092-1225, or visit her Web site at www.ritaherron.com.

Books by Rita Herron

†Nighthawk Island
*The Hartwell Hope Chests

CAST OF CHARACTERS

Olivia Thornbird—A reporter who wants to know the truth about her parents' deaths—even if it kills her.

Special Agent Craig Horn—A tough, hard-edged FBI agent without a conscience—until he meets Olivia Thornbird.

Dr. William Thornbird—Olivia's father died researching the strange virus killing innocent people in Savannah. But did he take the truth about the virus and his wife's death with him to his grave?

Dr. Ruth Thornbird—Her death twenty years ago was suspicious—could it be related to the current rash of virus/suicides in Savannah?

Senator Horn—Craig's father will do anything to protect his reputation, even keep secrets....

Dr. Hal Oberman—The Department of Public Safety's job is to protect the public. Is Dr. Oberman protecting himself instead?

Dr. Martin Shubert—He is suffering long-term effects of the virus that killed Olivia's mother—but was he responsible for the virus's creation?

Dr. Fred Fulton—Thornbird's coworker is racing against time to study the virus and create an antidote. Will he be able to do so in time to save Olivia?

DJ Dunce—A hired killer. But who is he working for, and why is he targeting Olivia?

Iskha Milaski—An internationally known terrorist, is he responsible for the virus that is being used to murder innocent people?

Prologue

Too many people had died already.

Ruth Thornbird had to tell someone the truth about what was going on. She'd come to this hellhole of a place hoping to help eradicate disease and had devoted her every day and night to the project, traveling to ungodly primitive areas to save lives.

But she'd been brought to Egypt under false pretenses. And three weeks into her mission, her orders had changed.

Now she was investigating a strange outbreak of an unnamed virus that was killing people in droves. A disease she suspected could have been prevented.

Worse, she also suspected innocent people were being used as test subjects without their knowledge.

Yanking the sterile gloves from her hands, she tossed them into the bin designated to collect biohazardous materials and rushed toward the small cubicle serving as her temporary office. Darkness bathed the cramped space, the desk lamp shedding the only light from a low-wattage bulb. The clock read nearly midnight. She'd purposely waited until everyone was gone so she wouldn't get caught.

Once she phoned the proper authorities and sent them her suspicious findings, she'd ask to return stateside. As much as she wanted to help cure this disease, for the first time in her life she actually feared what she might find—that there was no cure.

And that her own government was to blame for the outbreak.

Guilt slammed into her for being a coward and wanting to run, and she hesitated, but the angelic face of her eight-year-old daughter Olivia flashed in her mind, and her fingers tightened around the handset. She desperately wanted to hug her child. To forget that horrors like this existed.

The door squeaked open behind her. She jerked around, shocked to see a man enter and move into the shadows. Her nerves on edge, she searched his face for recognition, but he wore a surgical suit and mask. The only visible part of his body—his eyes.

They stared at her with a coldness that sent a chill down her spine.

"Who are you?" she asked.

"That doesn't matter," he said in a low voice. "But I can't let you leave here, Dr. Thornbird."

The low timbre of his tone made her stomach clench. She reached for her purse, but the man vaulted forward, knocked it from her hand, then manacled her wrist. When she saw the hypodermic in his hand, her blood turned to ice.

He lifted the needle so the tip glinted in front of her face. "You know what's in here, don't you?"

A sob caught in her throat. She not only knew, but she'd witnessed the deadly results of its effects. The bodies she'd been studying. The horrible way the people had suffered. The inevitable death.

Her heart pounding, she kicked out at him and ran, but he caught her, jabbed the needle into her neck, and held her until a chilling ache seeped through her. Her throat closed. Her body convulsed. The horrible panic of knowing what came next sliced through her.

She slumped to the floor like a rag doll as he released her.

Her little girl's face appeared in her mind's eye. Sweet, precious Olivia. That beautiful angelic blond hair. Those baby-blue eyes.

She'd talked to her husband earlier. Olivia was making posters, decorating the house for her homecoming. She'd been marking the days on the calendar until she returned. Had planned a surprise party with homemade chocolate chip cookies. Her husband was even taking the day off so they could all be together.

A tear rolled down her cheek, but she was helpless to wipe it away. Then she closed her eyes, welcoming the numbness. Regrets surfaced. She would never see her husband or baby girl again. Never hold them or kiss them good-night.

And no one would ever know the reason she'd died.

Chapter One

Fifteen years later

Olivia would find out the truth about the Savannah Suicides—even if it killed her. The local police and FBI couldn't just bury the story, hide the details from the public and get away with it.

Not like they had when her mother had died.

Bitterness threatened to rob her calm, but she stifled it. The only way to keep the world safe was to inform the people of potential dangers.

She swung her leather shoulder bag over her arm and marched toward the building that housed her father's office at CIRP, Coastal Island Research Park. She'd sensed he was keeping something from her the last few weeks. He'd been acting oddly secretive, distracted, had even sounded paranoid.

He'd even made some strange remarks about her mother's death and a cover-up, which he'd never spoken of before. And she thought he was working with the feds on the suicide cases.

She'd noticed an odd rash on two of the victims'

bodies at the crime scene and had spotted that federal agent, Craig Horn, leaving her father's office at least twice. She'd finally put two and two together. But when she'd contacted Agent Horn, he'd refused her calls. She'd tried to deal with the infuriating man before.

But Horn was cold. Calculating. An agent single-minded in his mission. A man with no feelings.

Her cell phone jolted out the programmed melody, and she answered it as she climbed into her Toyota. "Olivia Thornbird."

"Miss Thornbird, this is Special Agent Craig Horn of the FBI."

Olivia's eyebrows shot up. So, the sexy, enigmatic agent had finally decided to make her an ally. "I'm glad you called, Agent Horn. Are you ready to talk to me?"

A hesitant pause fraught with tension followed. "Miss Thornbird, I think you'd better get over to your father's house. He's barricaded himself inside."

"What?" Olivia's heart raced.

"I hate to tell you this," Agent Horn said in a decidedly low voice, "but you should hurry. He has a gun, and he's threatening to kill himself."

CRAIG DISCONNECTED the call, his hands sweating as he skimmed the overgrown yard surrounding Thornbird's small brick ranch. The sagging boards on the front porch attested to the house's age, the chipped paint, shutters hanging askew and dead plants evidence of lack of upkeep. Thornbird had first impressed him as a genius, scatterbrained scientist who related more to test tubes and vials than humans. He supposed it followed that he'd neglect his home for work, but this lack of long-term care indicated depression.

After meeting with Thornbird a few times, he guessed he and his daughter weren't close. The realization that Olivia's family had been just as screwed up as his own had spiked his curiosity about the woman and her drive. He actually admired her ambition.

If she wasn't a damn reporter, he might even like her.

And he sure as hell had to admit she was a looker.

But he'd never trust her.

The hushed murmurs of police officers communicating via radio jolted him back to reality. Several local police were situated at various strategic points around Thornbird's property, each armed and ready to bring this ordeal to a peaceful resolution. Others had cordoned off the property to contain neighbors, curious spectators and reporters.

Unfortunately, so far, Thornbird wasn't responding to their negotiation tactics. But at least he hadn't opened fire again like he had at Horn when he'd first arrived.

Craig raised the bullhorn one more time in an effort to defuse the increasingly catastrophic situation inside. "Dr. Thornbird, it's Craig Horn again. Please, sir, put down the gun, and let's talk."

"Go away, you communists! Leave me alone!" Thornbird shouted. "You're all just pagans wanting to steal the life from me and all the innocent people in this town."

"No, Dr. Thornbird. We've been working together, remember?"

The window suddenly shattered and the lights flickered off. Two cops raised their guns as if to fire, but Craig motioned for them to hold off.

"What's the story?" New arrivals to the scene, local cops Detective Adam Black and his partner, Clayton Fox, strode up and hunkered down beside him.

Craig filled them in. "Thornbird, the research scientist who's been studying the rash on our suicide vics, is holed up inside, threatening to kill himself."

"He find out anything about the rash?" Black asked.

"He thinks it's symptomatic of a virus, but he hadn't yet isolated the strain or determined its cause." Horn frowned as a breeze stirred the nearly dead leaves of the fern hanging from the front porch awning. "The last two weeks, he's been working day and night. I thought he might be on to something."

Fox raised a brow. "And?"

"A few days ago he started refusing my calls," Craig answered. "When I finally got through, he sounded disoriented. Paranoid."

Black's gaze met his. "All symptoms the other victims exhibited before they ended their lives."

Horn nodded, agitation constricting his stomach. Had Thornbird contracted the unnamed disease he'd been investigating?

Guilt nagged at him. He'd gotten the man involved. If Thornbird committed suicide, his death would rest on Craig's shoulders.

Suddenly the squeal of tires on asphalt jarred the tense silence, the air vibrating with the smell of burned rubber and panic as the car screeched to a stop. Olivia Thornbird jumped out and ran toward him. The sassy, confident air she normally wore had disintegrated since his call, the frantic unease of a terrified daughter flaring in her overly bright eyes instead.

The wind whipped her long blond hair around her face, and she scraped it back with a shaky hand, then reached for the bullhorn. "What did you do to him?"

He ignored her barb, plastered on a steely, cool face. "I've been trying to talk to him."

She glared at him. "He's been working for you, hasn't he?"

Craig swallowed hard, debating a lie. "He's been doing some research, yes."

"I knew it!" She grabbed the speaker and faced the house. "I have to talk to him."

Craig covered her hand with his. "I've made every attempt to convince him to come out, but he's incoherent."

Her gaze locked with his, then her bottom lip quivered slightly as his warning registered. Finally, she swung back toward the window, her bravado tacked in place. "Dad." Her voice warbled through the speaker. "It's me, Livvy."

Craig caught the anxious looks on the other cops' faces. They'd been down this same road too many times the past few weeks and lost. Hope wasn't exactly lighting the skies that this time would be any different.

"Dad, please come out, I'm worried about you."

"I can't."

"Dad, please, the police won't hurt you, I promise."

"I can't leave the house." His voice screeched. "It's the only place that's safe."

Olivia inhaled a deep breath. "Then let me come in and talk to you. Whatever's going on, we'll figure it out."

The curtains at the front window rustled open, and Craig spotted the old man peer through the broken glass. His wiry graying hair was standing on end, as if he'd run his hands through it a thousand times; his eyes appeared glassy, and his expression disoriented. "Ruth, is that you?"

"No, Dad." Anguish made her voice brittle. "It's me, Livvy. Mom's not here anymore, remember?"

"Livvy?"

"Yes. I'm coming in now. We'll talk, work out whatever is bothering you." She stepped forward tentatively.

"Livvy, no, stop! It's too dangerous! They're everywhere."

She took another cautious step. "Who's everywhere, Dad?"

"The spies," he cried. "They're on the lawn, in the house, on the roof. They'll get you."

"Dad, nothing's going to get me. I'm coming in."

"You don't understand." He waved his arm frantically in front of the window. "The government wants it kept quiet. I can't protect you anymore."

Olivia dashed forward, shoving away from Craig when he grabbed her arm. "Dad, it's okay. I'm right here, I'm coming in…."

Thornbird suddenly disappeared behind the wooden frame of the house, and Craig's instincts kicked in. "Olivia, stop!"

A gunshot pierced the air.

Olivia screamed and vaulted forward, but Craig caught her. He didn't have to go inside to know Thornbird was dead.

And it was all his fault.

"Noooo!" OLIVIA'S LEGS buckled as the guttural protest tore from her throat. Grief and shock welled inside her, overflowing. People shouted, officers mumbled and chaos erupted around her. Doubling over, she crumpled to the ground, but Agent Horn caught her as the police rushed into her father's house. Sobs racked her body, the tears spilling over, the anguish so deep she couldn't contain it.

Her father, the only family she had left, had just shot himself.

She clutched the agent's shirt, dazed and confused and too weak to stand. Horn stroked her hair and back, rocking her in his arms as he coaxed her to the front porch where she collapsed onto the stoop.

"Damn you, Horn," she exploded, jerking at his shirt, "this is all your fault. If you'd called me sooner, maybe I could have saved my dad. Why did you get him involved in this case?"

He clenched her wrists to stop her assault, but she lurched up and tore away from him, determined to see her father. Maybe he was still alive…

He grabbed her, yanked her back. "No, Olivia!"

"I have to see him. He might still make it!" Shoving him with all her might, she pushed past the police through the front door and into the foyer where she'd greeted her father so many times. The familiar details of the house registered—the same yellowed walls, the oak rolltop desk, the potted plant she'd given him for Christmas, now dead.

Then she spotted him lying on the faded beige carpeting. Face up, his jacket was open, his mouth gaping, his eyes glazed over in death. Blood splattered the floor, the walls, the charcoal gray suit he always wore, even his hands. A shotgun lay beside him, blood dotting the barrel.

The room spun. The stench of death and foul body odors assaulted her. The reality that this wasn't a story she was working on, but her own flesh and blood, hit her.

Mindless of what she was doing or saying, she dropped to her knees and cradled his hand in hers. "Daddy, please don't die," she whispered. "Please. I need you."

But the limp hand that met hers told her it was too late. Her father was already dead.

A FEW MOMENTS LATER, guilt churned at Craig as he dragged Olivia from her father. The EMT had already checked for a pulse while the police secured the scene and the CSI team rushed in.

He'd known Thornbird was behaving oddly, but hell, the man was strange, eccentric, had wanted to work on the case so much that he'd literally thrown himself into the job 24/7. Thornbird had never mentioned suicide though.

Or had Craig missed the signs?

Olivia's sobs finally quieted, but the glazed shock and pain in her eyes cut him to the bone.

"I'm sorry, Olivia." He rubbed her back to calm her, then gestured toward the kitchen which was visible from the small den but far enough to get her away from the body. "Come on, let's sit down."

She swayed as he guided her to a kitchen chair. Braced for another assault, Craig reached inside the battered cabinet, found a glass and filled it with tap water, then pressed it into her hand. "Drink this."

She obeyed, her acquiescence a definite sign of her devastation. Craig zeroed in on the details of the house.

It smelled old and musty, as if it hadn't been cleaned in ages. Haphazard piles of notes, medical magazines and journals cluttered every conceivable space. The furniture in the house looked Early American, all in golds and avocados, an obvious indication that Thornbird didn't value material wealth. He guessed the furniture had been early marriage. Other odors permeated the stale air—cigarette smoke, perspiration and rotting food. Fruit flies swarmed around two blackened bananas, and a dead fly floated in a glass of milk that had soured.

In the den, he spotted a yellowed photograph of Thornbird and a woman he assumed to be his wife. The woman had burnished copper hair instead of Olivia's gold, and it was straight, not wavy, but those killer blue eyes came from the same gene pool. The first picture was of their wedding. The next, the couple held an infant, obviously Olivia, in their arms, as they stood beside a faded green Chevrolet. Thornbird looked happy, content, so much younger that Craig barely recognized him.

The Thornbird he knew had empty eyes, and he'd never smiled. A strangled sound caught in Olivia's throat as she set the glass on the table, then she looked up at him with tears pooling in her baby-blue eyes.

"You got him involved in this," she said in a choked voice. "He got sick because he was investigating that rash for you, didn't he?"

He swallowed, aching for her, yet unwilling to show it. "I can't talk about the case."

She grabbed his shirt and shook him. "This is my father we're talking about, Agent Horn, not some anonymous stranger. He was working for you, and that job killed him."

Craig couldn't reply without compromising his case, but he couldn't argue with her, either.

Most people thought he was a coldhearted bastard. The Iceman, his co-workers called him.

Olivia thought the same, too. But he had to be the Iceman in order to do his job.

Just like he'd have to live with the guilt and the anguish in her eyes the rest of his life.

Chapter Two

As Craig checked on the progress of the investigation, his head rattled with questions about the rash, the possible virus and how the victims had contracted it.

Even more unsettling—how would they stop this illness from spreading and taking more lives if they didn't identify it soon? Worse, they'd have to keep things hush-hush to avoid a potential panic across the country.

Had the scientists at Nighthawk Island been researching the virus, or had they created it?

While the CSI team photographed the body and processed the crime scene area, the detectives were taking notes and talking in low voices.

"Canvass the neighbors," Detective Fox told two other officers. "See if anyone had a clue as to what Thornbird had planned or what was troubling him."

"Check and see if he had any recent visitors, too," Craig cut in. "I'll talk to his co-workers at CIRP."

Detective Black nodded and the men dispersed just as Agent Devlin approached him. "Did he give you any information about the research before he died?"

"No, but I'll question his colleagues, find someone

who understands his work and can pick up the thread where he left off," Craig said. "Maybe his files will aid in the identification process."

Devlin pocketed his cell phone and glanced at Olivia. "She going to be all right?"

Craig shrugged. "She's in shock."

Devlin nodded. "Don't suppose she'll be writing this one up."

Craig grimaced. True, but callous. He supposed it went with the agent's job. They'd both seen the darkest sides of life and survived. "She blames me for getting her old man involved."

"Don't go there, Horn. From what you told me, Thornbird volunteered to study this virus. I did some checking on the man. He was obsessed with his work. I think it had something to do with the way his wife died."

Craig arched his brows. "She died in Egypt, right?"

"Right. By another strange, unknown illness."

Craig picked up on Devlin's silent insinuation. "Did they do an autopsy?"

Devlin shook his head. "If they did, the results were never revealed. Authorities were too worried about transmitting the virus and refused to transport her body back to the States. She was cremated."

Craig swallowed hard. Maybe they were hiding something. "Must have been tough on the family."

"After that, Thornbird's reputation slid downhill. He lost a couple of grants and posts."

Craig's gaze swung to Olivia. Her face was so pale, her eyes listless, her arms wrapped around herself as if the muggy breeze blowing through the window might shatter her into pieces. He ordered himself to be impartial. This woman might be suffering now, but she'd been a pain in the butt wanting the scoop on his investigation. He couldn't afford to let her get too close.

Especially now.

She had even more reason to want the truth about the virus, even more reason to detest him and his unwillingness to cooperate.

"Listen, Horn." Devlin cleared his throat. "I received word this morning that two scientists have died in Germany. Their deaths sound remarkably similar to Thornbird's and our other suicide victims."

Craig frowned. The situation was desperate. They needed some answers fast. He hoped to hell Thornbird hadn't taken whatever information he'd learned concerning the virus to his grave.

DARKNESS SETTLED OVER Olivia's father's kitchen, the hushed voices and officers milling around the house echoing in the distant recesses of her mind like a TV she'd forgotten to turn off. Olivia blocked them out, unable to process the truth that her father was dead.

In her mind, she could see him standing by the scarred beige counter pouring his fifth cup of coffee into his favorite orange mug, one her mother had gotten for him in Portugal on one of her trips.

Through the back window, she watched the tire swing she used to spend hours in sway back and forth in the breeze, and the now defunct sandbox she'd played in as a child was covered with leaves and debris. The basketball hoop where she'd spent nights tossing the ball, thinking through stories she'd write for the school paper, was rusted, the net torn and ragged. Once her parents had planted flowers in that backyard, had grown herbs and roots, saying they didn't want her harmed by the processed foods and chemicals. They'd pushed Olivia in the swing, laughed as she'd run through the sprinkler, churned homemade ice cream on the patio while she'd learned to ride a bicycle.

Then her mother had died. And everything had changed.

There'd been no more laughing. No more homemade ice cream. No more herb garden.

Olivia had needed her father then. She'd begged him to let her crawl into his lap, but he'd pushed her away, as if he wished she'd died with her mother. Finally, she'd stopped trying to win his love.

But as a rebellious teenager she'd done other things to get his attention—misbehaved in school, gotten into scraps. She'd even ended up in jail for underage drinking and vandalizing. If her high school English teacher hadn't taken an interest in her and assigned her to the school paper, she would have ended up in the headlines more. But writing had given her a goal; a byline gained her the attention she'd been lacking.

Her stomach churned, her hands were sweating and her throat was so clogged with tears she felt as if a golf-ball had been lodged inside. Forcing herself to think rationally, like a reporter and not a grief-stricken daughter, she scanned the kitchen for clues to her father's mental state, searching for any changes in the room that might indicate what had brought him to the point of suicide.

Three coffee cups, a stack of used plates with dried bread crumbs and a half-eaten sandwich overflowed the sink. Cigarette ashes littered the top of a soda can, the fact that her father had partaken of both a testament to how much he'd changed.

Except for his work. That, he'd never ignored.

Not as he had her.

"Olivia?" Craig's voice made her spring back into action. She stood and walked toward him. "Was there a suicide note?"

He hesitated, then shook his head.

"I want to see his things, especially his desk."

The detective beside him cast Craig a warning look and strode toward another crime scene tech who was bagging the gun Olivia's father had used to shoot himself.

"Olivia, the police and FBI are working this case. Let us do our job."

She gripped his arm. "I have to know everything he was working on. He was obsessive-compulsive and would never have left a project unfinished."

"We'll find the answers," Craig said through gritted teeth. "Just give us time."

She narrowed her eyes, battling another onslaught of tears. She didn't want sympathy, she wanted the truth. "He died because of the work he was doing for you, didn't he? I saw you leaving his office—"

"Yes, he was helping us." A muscle twitched in his jaw. "But that's all I can say."

"I saw the red welts on the other victims," she said. "You think all the suicide victims had some kind of virus. What does it do—cause the infected people to go crazy?"

"I can't disclose details that might jeopardize the case, Olivia. You have to understand that."

She folded her arms, her anger rallying. "This isn't

just a case, Horn. It took my father's life. And what about more innocent lives that might be lost if you cover this up?"

"Don't you think I'm working my tail off to get to the truth so there won't be any more victims?"

She bit her lip. "If my father did contract some rare virus, it wasn't an accident. He was meticulous about safety precautions."

Craig's dark gray eyes met hers, silently acknowledging her declaration as he gestured around the den and kitchen. "Judging from the looks of his house, I might question that."

"It's usually not this bad. And he was much more precise and detailed about his work."

"Everyone makes mistakes, Olivia. A punctured glove, a spill, if he was dealing with some unknown bacteria he didn't recognize—"

"No," Olivia snapped. "He *never* made mistakes."

Except he hadn't pushed the government for the truth about her mother. When Olivia had gotten older and questioned him about her mother's death, he'd refused to answer. She'd realized then that he'd allowed the government to get away with their cover-up.

That was the reason she'd gone into journalism. Someone had buried the truth about her mother's death, and one day she hoped to uncover it. She sure as hell wouldn't let them bury the story about her father's death now, too.

"If my father contracted this virus," she said in a cold voice, "someone infected him."

Craig grimaced. "You're suggesting murder?"

"I'm suggesting this is some kind of germ or chemical warfare, and you're trying to keep it under wraps from the public." She ignored the flare of heat in his eyes. "But trust me, Agent Horn, I refuse to let my father's death go until I discover the truth."

"Trust you?" His voice dripped sarcasm. "I learned a long time ago not to trust reporters." His unwavering glare slid over Olivia. "I feel for you, Olivia, I honestly do. But I'm warning you—don't get in the way of this investigation."

Olivia shot him an equally menacing look. She'd be damned if she'd let him intimidate her.

They were both after the truth.

Unfortunately, they were on opposite sides.

CRAIG WAS ON THE VERGE of suggesting someone drive Olivia home when Dr. Ian Hall, the director of CIRP, rushed inside, accompanied by Detective Clayton Fox.

"I came as soon as I heard."

Hall's face looked ruddy with emotions, his tie hanging askew as if he'd been twisting it in the car. The sweltering summer heat drifting through the door also marked his skin with perspiration. "What happened?" Hall asked.

Craig gestured toward Olivia before explaining. "Dr. Hall, this is Olivia Thornbird, Dr. Thornbird's—"

"I know who she is." Hall's look bordered between a scowl and regret. "Miss Thornbird has been to my office several times in the past few months."

Craig nodded. "Of course." She would have been looking for a story. Or maybe she'd covered some of the disreputable events that had occurred at the research park already. He made a mental note to check the newspaper archives.

"It appears that my father killed himself," Olivia said before he could finish, "because of some research he was doing regarding the Savannah Suicides."

Hall's face blanched. "How do you know it had something to do with his work?"

"We don't," Craig said, vying for damage control. "The medical examiner will have to determine cause of death, and if Dr. Thornbird was suffering from any other medical problems." Craig indicated Thornbird's computer and the cluttered oak desk. "We are confiscating all of his research notes and hope you'll provide us with a liaison to interpret them."

Hall scraped a hand over his forehead. "Certainly. We'll do whatever we can to expedite the investigation."

Craig grunted. CIRP had a reputation for keeping certain projects classified, even from the feds. With the current state of the world and constant threat of terrorism, studying biological and chemical warfare had to rank at the top of their priorities. The security they enforced upon the employees and their research projects at Nighthawk Island was cutting-edge, but their secrecy suspicious.

Hall offered Olivia a conciliatory smile. "Miss Thornbird, please allow CIRP to pay the expenses for your father's burial. He was a valued employee of the scientific community and will be sorely missed."

Olivia's face paled at the mention of a funeral, and Craig was tempted to reach out and offer her a comforting hand, but she stiffened perceptibly when he stepped closer. "How valuable was he to you, Dr. Hall?" she asked.

Hall's eyes narrowed. "I'm not certain what you mean."

Olivia squared her shoulders. "I've heard about your

community and the founders of CIRP. They actually killed two of their scientists for nearly exposing secretive work you were conducting. Perhaps that's what happened to my father."

Hall squared his shoulders. "Any disreputable activities that occurred in the past are to be left there," he said curtly. "Since I assumed leadership of CIRP, things have changed. Recently one of our psychiatrists, Claire Kos, was instrumental in helping catch the serial killer stalking Savannah."

"But it's awfully coincidental that Savannah is suddenly stricken with something that might be a dangerous unknown virus when your team is conducting secretive research on Nighthawk Island." Olivia's voice held an undercurrent of accusations. "Perhaps my father discovered the truth about the rash these suicide victims had contracted. What if his findings lead back to CIRP? And you had him killed to keep him quiet?"

"You're letting your grief make you irrational." Hall's eyes flickered with anger. "And I wouldn't print false accusations like that in the paper, Miss Thornbird."

"Oh, I'll find proof to substantiate it before I print it."

A vein in Hall's forehead throbbed. "Your father shot himself, didn't he?"

"That is the apparent cause of death," Craig answered, in an attempt to defuse the volatile situation before it spiraled completely out of hand.

Olivia had a point, but so did Hall.

In fact, it had also occurred to him that Hall and the other scientists at CIRP might hurt Thornbird to keep him from discovering the truth about the virus.

Olivia's words rushed back to haunt him.

My father was meticulous about safety precautions. If he was infected, it wasn't accidental.

Could she be right? Could someone have infected Thornbird? If so, his suicide would be murder. And he had just asked Hall for a liaison to interpret the results…

Could Craig trust Hall and the next scientist, or would they alter results to cover for CIRP?

And what about Olivia—if she kept tossing out accusations, would she put herself in danger?

"OLIVIA, I'M GOING TO drive you home."

Olivia shook her head. "I'd like to stay here a while longer."

Craig's sharp gaze cataloged the chalk lines outlining the space where her father's body had fallen. The other cops were leaving, the house dusted and tattooed with the crime scene unit's handiwork. The spectators and reporters had given up and gone home, too. "Even if I could let you do that—and I can't," Craig said, "—it's not a good idea." He took her elbow as if to guide her to the door. "You're wiped out and need some rest."

Emotionally drained would be the more correct assessment. Dead inside even closer.

But she'd be damned if she'd admit any weakness to the federal agent who'd made her life hell the last few weeks. Even if he did have the sexiest gray eyes she'd ever seen. And even if for a brief moment, his ironclad control had slipped and concern tinged his voice.

"I…I can't leave," she whispered, betraying herself as her gaze caught sight of the wedding photo of her father and mother on the end table by the couch. The realization that she was all alone in the world slammed into her with such force that the breath locked in her lungs.

"Is there someone I can call?" he asked quietly. "A family member? Friend? Boyfriend?"

"No...no one." She swallowed back tears at how pathetic it all was. Just like her father, she'd drowned herself in work at the expense of forming close friendships. And she couldn't remember the last time she'd had a date.

Emotions suddenly choked her, and she turned away, embarrassed and determined to regain control. "You don't have to take care of me, Agent Horn."

"Yes, I do."

His gruff words hung in the air, thick with concern. Whatever his intention—to spy on her or offer her a semblance of comfort—guilt also riddled his voice.

She didn't want his guilt or pity.

"I have my car," she said, swinging back around. "I drove myself here. I can drive myself home."

"Miss Independent, huh? You never need anyone, right?"

"That's right."

His gaze locked with hers, the day's events traipsing through her mind like a bad headline. Tomorrow, her father's suicide would be splattered across the papers. She'd need to make plans for the funeral. Think about a burial plot. A memorial service. A casket.

That is, when the medical examiner finally released the body.

It was all too much.

Feeling weak-kneed, she scrounged in her purse for her keys, but Horn placed his hand over hers. "I'm taking you home, Olivia. No arguments. If you want to come back tomorrow, I'll bring you to get your car. But you're not driving right now."

For once in her life, she was too exhausted to argue, so she nodded and followed him to his nondescript sedan. The interior was clean, cool, unwelcoming— just like the man.

She gave him directions to the apartment she rented, one half of an older house that had been converted into duplexes. The night sounds and lights of Savannah passed by in a blur. Blues music floated from Emmet Park where locals often gathered to jam, the rumble of traffic and Saturday-night partygoers and tourists flooding River Street, reminding her that, although she was grieving, life went on.

Down the street, two lovers walked hand in hand, enjoying the moonlight. Another couple laughed as they strolled with their baby.

She fumbled with her keys and climbed out, ignoring Horn when he followed her onto the stoop. Her hand trembled as she inserted the key and opened the door, a well of darkness greeting her from the inside, the happy couples a reminder of a life she might never have.

Craig Horn's gruff voice broke the quiet. "Olivia, are you going to be all right?"

The heat from the apartment felt like a sweltering oven, the bleak emptiness threatening to swallow her whole.

No, she'd never be okay again.

But she nodded anyway. Just as she started to step inside, Craig caught her arm. She glanced at his fingers where they were pressed into her bare skin, the brief contact sending a tingling up her body that stirred another kind of heat.

God, she was hurting tonight. And she was so alone.

His arms would be so strong around her. If just for the night.

For a brief moment, they simply stood there, the anguish and horror of her father's suicide a link between them, the guilt and nature of their jobs a barrier that stood in the way.

"I'm sorry," he finally said in a strained voice.

She swallowed, unable to reply or to force herself inside just yet. He traced his finger down her arm, over the top of her hand. Her breath caught at the tenderness. She nearly opened her fingers and laced them with his to pull him into the darkness with her, to ask him to take away the pain.

Instead, she remained still, her emotions waging a silent battle. She couldn't get hurt if she didn't get involved. And she couldn't ask for help or comfort…

He suddenly released her as if he'd felt the connection and didn't like it, either. With a grim expression, he reached inside his pocket and withdrew a business card. The Iceman had returned.

"This is my work number, and here's my home number and cell. Call me if you need anything." His gaze locked with hers again, his voice husky. "I mean it, Olivia. Any time, day or night."

She accepted the card, their fingers touching briefly, tempting her again. His masculine scent wafted toward her, teasing, erotic, eliciting images of hands and bodies touching.

But she summoned her courage and walked inside without bothering to reply. After all, they both knew that she wouldn't call.

Olivia Thornbird couldn't lean on anyone.

Especially Craig Horn, the man who'd gotten her father killed.

Chapter Three

The anguish in Olivia's eyes haunted Craig while he drove to the cabin he'd rented on Skidaway Island. He'd wanted to go inside, to hold her, to kiss her, to soothe her pain.

But he couldn't take advantage of her grief.

Then he'd be an even worse kind of bastard than he already was.

After all, he was responsible for her father's death.

Frustrated at his weakness for the sexy woman, he opened the windows, welcoming the heat. When Devlin had first asked him to relocate to Savannah a few weeks before to investigate Nighthawk Island, he'd been grateful for the reprieve of the coast and warm sunshine. After years of living in Washington D.C., dealing with politics and the accompanying red tape, along with city traffic, noise and crime, he'd thought the job would be a picnic.

Though the scenery had changed and the pace of the southern town was much slower than the capital city, gaining access to Nighthawk Island's secretive projects was just as difficult as infiltrating street gangs or corrupt politicians' offices.

Exhausted, he yanked off his tie, tossed it onto the faded sofa in the den, flipped on the lamp which sprayed the room in a watery dim light, then opened the French doors. The sounds of the ocean crashing against the shore burst into the room, the high tide rising to wash away the remnants of sand castles built earlier.

The first day when he'd arrived he'd noticed the happy families vacationing, the babies in sunbonnets, the toddlers digging in the sand with big plastic shovels, the mothers chasing them to the edge of the water, the fathers tossing their kids into the waves and catching them as they squealed in delight. He'd tried to remember if his own family had ever vacationed like that, spending lazy days strolling on the beach gathering seashells and romping.

His memories consisted of formal dinner parties, being scolded if he tracked dirt on the marble foyer, eating with the housekeeper while his parents campaigned across the state, then later across the country.

And then his sister's death... It had torn the family even further apart. Especially the family's refusal to talk about it. It was almost as if his sister had never existed, as if she'd been wiped out like words on a chalkboard that had been erased. At family dinners and holidays no one even bothered to mention her name. Not that there were many family holidays or dinners...

An image of Thornbird's face, bloody and pale with death, floated back, and he grimaced.

Although he hadn't spoken to his dad in months, the urge to call him sent Craig to the phone, but he hesitated, his fingers lingering over the handset. His father's parting words echoed in his mind. "You fool! You let a woman trick you into getting information on me. She nearly ruined my career."

Just as it was his fault that Olivia's father had died tonight.

He dropped his hand from the receiver. His father had never forgiven him.

Olivia wouldn't, either.

Another reason some agents called him the Iceman. The end always justified the means. He'd use anyone he had to in order to get a job done. And if someone died in the process, hell, it was just a loss they had to take.

OLIVIA POURED HERSELF a glass of merlot, slipped on a nightshirt and opened the window in her bedroom, welcoming the sultry heat from the summer air while she desperately tried to banish memories of her father's lifeless body from her mind.

The phone rang, shrill in the night, and she answered it, hoping it would be Agent Horn with some answers. Or maybe she just wanted to hear his husky voice.

God, she was desperate….

Her boss's deep baritone boomed instead. "Olivia, it's Carter. So sorry to hear about your father."

She cleared her throat. "Thanks, it…was a shock."

"What happened?"

She hesitated, wondered whether to share her suspicions yet. "I don't know. He was depressed lately, was agitated, but he hadn't confided any specifics."

"Do you think his death is related to the other suicides?"

"I don't know. I spoke to Agent Horn, but he was closemouthed."

"He's a cold one, all right."

Yes. Except he hadn't been tonight.

"You're not giving up, though?"

"No." She saw her father's face in her mind. Remembered her resolve about her mother. "Definitely not."

"Good, I know there's a story there. I suspect it has to do with Nighthawk Island, too. If you can get it, your career will be made."

For a fleeting second, she didn't care about her career. "Lowell, I don't intend to sensationalize my father's death for a byline."

"That's not what I meant. But everyone is trying to get the truth about the shady research at Nighthawk Island, and you might just be the one to uncover it."

Right.

She hung up, troubled by the conversation. If Nighthawk Island was keeping secrets about her father's work and one of those projects was creating public danger, she had an obligation to inform the innocent citizens. She couldn't sit back and let the truth be buried as it had been when her mother died years ago.

In fact, her father had mentioned her mother at least a half dozen times lately. He'd even claimed that someone might be listening over the phone when they'd last talked.

What if someone *had* been listening? Someone who hadn't wanted him to finish researching the virus?

She swirled the red liquid in her glass, willing the rich flavor to dull the pain that coursed through her soul. All these years, she'd hoped for answers. Prayed that one day she and her father would be close again. That he'd wake up and see the daughter he'd forgotten existed. And maybe, in some way, she'd thought by making a name for herself in the paper, by getting bigger headlines, uncovering important stories, putting herself on the line, that he'd take notice.

That dream had died today, as well.

Tears spilled over her cheeks, the black abyss of her sorrow too much to bear, and she finally crawled beneath the covers of her bed, doubled over and released the pent-up emotions she'd been bottling so long. Heartrending sobs escaped her.

She would never be any closer to her father than she had been the day her mother had died. Would never fully understand the reason he'd virtually abandoned her for test tubes and research files.

But she would know the answers to the reason he'd died.

Special Agent Craig Horn's face drifted into her mind. Sharp chiseled features. A strong jawbone. Black hair that framed a face that had seen hard times. Eyes as gray as a granite sky or the fog that enveloped the island after a storm.

His voice, his expression, his manner—it had always seemed so cold. Distant.

The Iceman. She'd heard the rumors about the other agents thinking he was nothing but a tomb, devoid of emotion.

And she'd understood why.

Yet today, his hand had been gentle when he'd brushed hers. So gentle she'd ached for more. For him to stroke her face, caress her body, touch his lips to hers. Give her comfort in the heat of this sorrowful night.

She hated herself for wanting him.

Another sob erupted from deep inside her throat, and she gave in to it. She was alone. No one would hear. No one would know how weak she really was.

But tomorrow, she'd pull herself together. She'd comb every inch of CIRP, pester Craig Horn and Ian Hall to death, even sneak onto Nighthawk Island if she had to. But she'd find out the truth.

And no one, not the Savannah police or the FBI or Craig Horn, the Iceman, would make her change her mind.

REGARDLESS OF THE LATE HOUR, when Agent Devlin showed up at Craig's door, they spread the files on the Savannah Suicides on the wooden desk and studied the information collected so far.

Devlin read aloud, "The first victim: Damon Byrd. Twenty-seven. A local banker. Single. Lived alone. Had a girlfriend named Tia. She claimed they broke up three weeks before the man died."

Craig tapped his pen on the desk, then picked up where Devlin had left off. "Tia said her boyfriend had been exhibiting erratic behavior the last few weeks, had been temperamental, had become physically violent. Co-workers corroborated her story. Normally an easygoing, quiet man who got along with everyone, no one had any clue as to what had caused the change in the man's behavior. Two days before he died, his boss had ordered him to see a psychiatrist. He'd also given him two weeks leave to deal with his issues. If he didn't, he'd be fired."

"Break up with girlfriend. Job problems," Devlin summarized. "That might lead to suicide. But what caused the behavior change?"

Craig frowned. "Money problems, maybe?" He searched the reports and found financial statements, quickly skimming aloud the man's net worth, debt and recent credit card statements, but found no significant financial problems.

"Interesting," Devlin said. "If anything, Damon Byrd was a prime example of solid investments with a sizable savings account and a decent stock portfolio, although his cumulative worth wasn't significant enough to warrant murder."

"And all signs point to suicide," Craig said. "According to the medical examiner's report, Byrd shot himself in the head at close range with a .38 which had been registered in his name. He'd purchased it a few weeks before." Craig skimmed further. "Do you think it's possible the victims belonged to some kind of cult?"

"One that made a suicide pact?" Devlin asked.

Craig nodded.

"I'll put someone on that angle," Devlin said, "although there's no references to either one of them joining any kind of religious or activist type group."

"Maybe those lab results will help pinpoint the nature of this virus," Craig said. "Thornbird was probably waiting on those reports as well."

"There has to be some connection we're missing." Devlin scratched his chin. "Victim two. Emmett Grayson, forty years old. Married. Two kids in high school. Worked as a garage mechanic."

Craig twisted his mouth in thought. "So far, no similarities."

"Except that his wife, neighbors and co-workers all said his behavior had changed. He seemed angry all the time, had even threatened to hit his son, had slammed his fist through a window at the garage when a disgruntled client accused him of overcharging for services."

"The erratic behavior change," Craig said. "It has to be a result of the virus. Maybe it's spreading through some kind of chemical spill that was absorbed in the water or land," Craig said.

"Water samples have come back clean." Devlin shuffled the papers. "Still waiting on the results of the soil samples."

"There's another possibility we have to consider," Devlin said. "The victims might have been targets."

"You mean someone purposely infected them?" Craig scrubbed a hand over his day's growth of beard stubble. "What's the motive?"

"I'm not sure. Thornbird could have been killed to stop the research. As far as a connection, the two vics in Europe were also scientists, but the first two victims here weren't, so I don't see a connection between them." Devlin gathered his notes. "I'm leaving for Germany in the morning to conference with the agents there. You're in charge here."

Craig accessed the Internet when Devlin left, then checked for stories with Olivia's byline. She'd penned a piece about the original director of CIRP who'd died after conducting unethical experiments and trying to sell research to a foreign government. And she'd covered the end of the Savannah serial killings and the attack on Claire Kos.

But so had the other papers, and her piece hadn't revealed details not also covered in the other papers.

Outside, the tide had begun to break, the resounding echo of the waves fading to a soft lull. Mosquitoes buzzed at the window, a muggy breeze bringing the odor of fish and salt water. His mind shifted back to the families on the beach earlier, and he walked back to the open French doors. The soft halo of the moon bathed the sand, and a lone couple strolled hand in hand along the edge of the water, their soft laughter tinkling in the night.

Olivia Thornbird's face flashed into his mind. For a brief moment, he allowed himself to forget that he was a trained agent, a man who was supposed to live without feelings, a man who'd spent time overseas in secret military missions that he'd never discuss with anyone. A man who refused to get involved with a woman because emotions interfered with his job.

He let himself imagine he and Olivia walking the beach, lingering in the shadow of the moon with heated touches and erotic kisses. But the sound of her heart-rending cries bled into the darkness.

Those cries would stay with him tonight. And probably forever.

He was a genius.

A harsh laugh rumbled deep in his chest as he recalled the stumped looks on the policemen's faces when they'd stood outside Thornbird's house and heard that gunshot blast. And when they'd seen the rash…oh, he wished he'd had a camera. They were chasing their tails to discern how he'd accomplished what he had.

But they would never figure out the truth. Not all of it, anyway.

He crushed the seashells in his hand, then scattered the broken pieces across the grass, smiling as blood trickled down his palm. Instead of wincing at the pain, he relished it, had been trained to endure it, in fact. It drove him. Made him the man he was.

He stared at Olivia Thornbird's dark apartment, wondering about the woman inside. She was beautiful. Tenacious. Smart.

Would Olivia Thornbird be manipulated by the puppet master himself?

Probably. All he wanted was for her to print the story. Stir panic. Do her job.

And she wouldn't be able to resist.

Yet, he suspected the master might have underestimated her inquisitive nature.

Soundlessly, he moved into the shadows of the live oak as a couple strolled by on the sidewalk. His boss had been watching her father for some time. Wondering if eventually he'd let his ethics and conscience get to him again. And when the feds had enlisted Thornbird's help, he'd known he had to do something fast before Thornbird unearthed the truth.

The traffic noises in the background jarred the quiet, but he blocked it out as he had learned to do with all sensory intrusions.

A light flickered on in Olivia's bedroom, and he glanced up at the window, unease tickling his spine when her silhouette appeared in the window. Pain would only cause Olivia Thornbird to push harder, just as it had him.

Though she'd disagree, they were very much alike.

She wouldn't let things rest. Unfortunately, if she dug too deeply into the past, he'd have to take care of her, too. Just as he had the others.

But not tonight.

The master would tell him when the time was right.

Chapter Four

Olivia awakened the next morning with a heavy ache in her chest. Her father was gone, and there were dozens of arrangements to make for his funeral.

But she lacked the energy for any of them.

Besides, it would take time for the medical examiner to complete the autopsy. Longer than normal, especially if Agent Horn was doing his job. They would conduct a battery of tests on his body that would be extensive, involve sending samples away to various labs for analysis and cross-referencing with other databases for cases that might be similar.

She needed to get into the house and look through her father's files before Agent Horn returned and confiscated them. If he hadn't already.

She poured herself a strong cup of coffee, grabbed the morning paper, and nearly choked over the photograph of her father's limp body lying on the floor.

Her co-worker and competitor, Jerry Renard, had written the piece, slanting the article as she would have, raising questions about the correlation with the other so-called suicides.

Fueled by his comments and knowing that if she

didn't get the real story, someone else would, someone who might paint her father in a poor light, she phoned the Department of Public Safety.

"Miss Thornbird," the receptionist said in a derisive tone, "Dr. Oberman is not accepting calls from reporters."

"Tell him that I'm not just any reporter, I'm the daughter of the latest victim of the Savannah Suicides, that I'm not going away until he talks to me, that—"

"One moment please."

Olivia tapped the table with her fingernails while she waited. It seemed like forever before a man came on the line. "Miss Thornbird, Dr. Oberman."

"Finally."

"Listen, young lady, I'm a very busy man—"

"Hopefully trying to find out what's causing the virus that's prompting these suicides in Savannah. I want to know what you're doing to protect the public."

He coughed, obviously surprised at her boldness. "First of all, I have spoken with the federal agents working the case, and they've assured me everything possible is being done to get to the bottom of these suicides. There is no proof that a virus has anything to do with the cases."

"That's bull and you know it. My father was a scientist who worked for CIRP. He was consulting with Special Agent Craig Horn about the virus."

"He told you that?"

Olivia hedged. "Yes. And before his death, my father exhibited the same symptoms as the other victims."

"Miss Thornbird, I can assure you that if there is some connection, our federal agents will find it. Now, please let the police do their jobs, and don't create widespread panic by printing unsubstantiated speculations."

"Dr. Oberman, fifteen years ago, my mother also died of a suspicious virus she contracted while working for the government. When my father asked questions, he hit a dead end because your people covered it up." Angry, her voice rose an octave. "I don't intend for my father's death to be swept under the rug like hers. Both of them were working for *you*. Now find out what killed them and let me know what you're doing to protect the public, or when I find out, and I *will*, I'll expose all of your dirty little secrets and blow you clean out of office."

Furious, she slammed down the phone, inhaled her coffee and washed down a chocolate candy bar for breakfast, her vice when she was upset.

The phone rang. Expecting the caller to be Oberman, she picked it up, fuming. "I meant what I said—don't mess with me."

"If I were you, I wouldn't be making threats, or you'll wind up like your father."

Olivia froze, the handset clenched between clammy fingers. The caller's voice was deeper than Oberman's, maybe even simulated.

"Who is this?"

"I'm warning you, Miss Thornbird, stay out of the way or you'll regret it."

She opened her mouth to speak again, but the phone clicked into silence.

"AGENT HORN, I just received a call from Olivia Thornbird."

Craig silently cursed. Dr. Oberman, head of the DPS, sounded royally pissed.

Damn it. He'd barely gotten out of the shower and there were already more problems. He shook the water from his hair, knotted a towel around his waist and went to the kitchen for more coffee. "I can't say I'm surprised. The woman is persistent."

"*Persistent?* Hell, she's a bomb ready to explode." Oberman released a string of expletives. "What's the situation?"

"So far, all the vics have shown symptoms of a rash, red patchy skin, fever and nosebleeds, prior to death, as well as symptoms of depression. There are too many similarities for the individual cases to be coincidence. We're trying to find a connection."

"The bottom line, Horn? Are these suicides?"

"Yes and no. For now, we're calling them suicides, at least that's what we're telling the press."

"What the hell does that mean?"

"It means that, technically, each of the victims took his own life. But we believe that the virus causes psychotic behavior which drives them to kill themselves."

"That's the damnedest thing I've ever heard."

"But a perfect front for murder. We're looking at three possibilities—a cult, a serial killer or a terrorist faction, although if this is a serial killer, we haven't documented any similar cases before. And we have no evidence showing that any of the victims belonged to a cult."

Oberman swore.

Craig continued, "We also don't know how the virus is being contracted, if it's contagious and why these people have been targeted."

"Hell, if it is a terrorist group, there may be no rhyme or reason."

"But if we find out how these folks are getting the virus, we can pinpoint who might be spreading it and if they are being infected intentionally."

"You've checked the water and soil?" Oberman asked.

"Still have some tests pending."

"Is the virus airborne?"

"No. And so far, samples from the first victim's home showed no contamination." Although they hadn't finished testing Thornbird's work clothes.

"Well, that's a relief."

"Yes. Thornbird was working on isolating the virus when he died. I'm having his research analyzed."

Oberman groaned. "So Olivia Thornbird was right? Her father was working for you."

"Yes." The knot of anxiety in Horn's chest tightened. "Now we have to start over with a new scientist, Dr. Fred Fulton. Dr. Ian Hall, the director of CIRP, says he's cooperating. But I'm not certain we can trust either of them."

"Have duplicate tests run. Samples sent to the CDC in Atlanta. I'll speak to the higher-ups there and tell them to expect it."

"Right." Craig explained about Devlin's visit to Europe.

Oberman hissed, "I don't want this story leaked. I'm worried about Olivia Thornbird."

"I'll handle her."

"Good, do whatever it takes," Oberman barked.

Craig frowned and hung up, wondering what Oberman had meant.

Olivia's anguished expression returned to haunt him. Could he do whatever it took to keep her quiet?

He'd have to shut her out. Lie to her. Pretend he didn't

give a damn about her old man, that his research hadn't gotten him killed.

Which they both knew was a lie.

But that would be the easy part. After all, he was FBI. The Iceman. Keeping things undercover and lying were an inherent part of the job.

The hard part would be resisting Olivia's tempting lips and bewitching eyes.

ALTHOUGH OLIVIA WAS SHAKEN by the phone call, the warning only confirmed what she already suspected—that somebody had intentionally infected her father with the virus.

That his research was the key to the rash of suicides in Savannah, and that technically now the others might be related. That they might not be suicides at all.

Her fingers slid over the card Agent Horn had given her the night before with his invitation to phone if she needed him. Should she tell him about the threat?

Maybe.

But not yet.

After all, what could he do? The caller hadn't talked long enough for a trace. And he'd been calling from an unlisted number. Besides, if she told Craig, he'd insist she have some protection.

She couldn't do her job with someone watching over her shoulder.

She phoned for a cab, hurried outside and waited for it, then quickly instructed the driver where to go.

A few minutes later, the driver parked at her father's house, and turned to her, his bushy eyebrows raised. "Ain't that the house where that man shot himself yesterday?"

Olivia nodded, unwilling to elaborate.

He smacked his rubbery lips. "Thought that yellow tape meant to stay out."

She rolled her eyes, her patience thin. "Just let me out."

He grumbled, then accepted her money, eyeing the tip as if he expected more, so she stuffed an extra five dollars in his hand, hoping he wouldn't mention his drop-off to anyone.

Feeling jittery but determined, she slipped beneath the tape, hurried around to the back door, unlocked it and dashed inside. She wanted to be alone in the house. Have time to remember her father and to search through his files.

A few minutes later, she sighed in defeat. Of course, the FBI had confiscated his computer and diskettes. They'd also searched his desk.

On the off chance he might have hidden information, she went into his bedroom. The scent of cigarette smoke and her father's cologne assaulted her, bringing a surge of sadness. Her father's favorite plaid shirt lay on the floor, and the worn soles of his loafers peeked from beneath the unmade bed. A stack of medical journals were stacked haphazardly on the floor in one corner, a half dozen notepads scattered across the bed.

She thumbed through each one, looking for notes. But the pages were empty. Frustrated, she opened her father's closet in search of a file box that might hold disks or information, but didn't find one. Her father's lab coat lay on the floor, memories of watching him shrug into it filling her head. She picked it up, pressed it to her cheek and inhaled her father's scent, for a brief moment allowing nostalgia to sweep her back in time.

Seconds later, she fought the grief and forced herself to search the pockets. Inside, she found a small scrap of paper. Curious, she unfolded it, her eyes widening as she read.

Dr. Thornbird, if you don't back off, you're dead.

KNOWING OLIVIA WOULD WANT her car back, Craig phoned her, but when she didn't answer, he assumed she'd already gone to her father's.

Not a good idea.

The agents had searched the house already, but she would undoubtedly want to do so herself. And there was the possibility that she might know places to look that they didn't.

He shouldn't have left her alone for a second. Might even need to put a tail on her.

He jumped in his car and phoned the coroner's office while he drove toward Thornbird's.

"We're starting to work on Thornbird today," Dr. Rollins said.

"I spoke with Dr. Oberman from the DPS. He wants duplicate samples sent to the CDC in Atlanta for a crosscheck. Devlin will also have samples of any cultures taken from the European scientists sent there to compare. And send duplicate samples to CIRP."

Rollins agreed, and he hung up, then turned down the drive to Thornbird's. His gut told him Olivia was already here.

And that she'd bypass the yellow tape and go inside.

Not that he could blame her. She was intelligent. The man's daughter. She had reason to be suspicious.

But she could screw up this investigation badly. And if they discovered there was a serial killer, if this was some kind of terrorist attack or if CIRP was involved, secrecy would be their best defense.

The neighborhood looked different today without the curious neighbors and the police cars parked on the side. Although the immediate threat of violence had dissipated on the surface, had the residents locked their doors last night? Been suspicious of their neighbors? Warned their children not to ride their bikes outside their drives?

Their peace would be destroyed if his suspicions were confirmed or if Olivia printed her own in the paper.

He scanned the exterior of the house. Nothing looked amiss. Her car was still in the same spot. No lights were on inside.

He approached cautiously. Decided to check the back before he went inside.

He walked around the overgrown yard, noticed the tire swing, the area where a garden had once been. Thought of the family that had once lived there. The one that was now gone.

And then he glanced through the back bedroom window and saw Olivia.

Her blond hair spilled around her shoulders, the dark circles beneath her eyes a testament to a grief-spent night.

His gut clenched as he thought about her carrying the burden of her father's loss all alone.

Do whatever you have to do to keep her quiet, Oberman had ordered.

He braced himself to do just that as he reached for the door.

OLIVIA CLAMPED HER LIP over her teeth at the sight of Craig Horn. Last night outside her apartment door, the air had grown tight around them. The memory of his hands on her, stroking her, holding her, had come unbidden during the night. And with the morning sunlight glinting off his bronzed cheeks, he looked more handsome than any federal agent had a right to be. More like a renegade than FBI.

But he worked for the government. He was the enemy. And gone was any hint of gentleness. The hardassed, stone-cold Iceman was back.

"Olivia, you know you shouldn't be in here."

"I…I need clothes for my father for the funeral."

He arched a dark brow. "The medical examiner is nowhere near releasing your father's body."

"I have to sort through his things."

His eyes darkened as if he suspected she was lying. "So soon?"

"Yes. I…need to do it."

"You mean you need to check out his work? Look for some clue as to why he'd take his life?"

"Wouldn't you if you were in my shoes and your father had died?"

He silently cursed. At one time, he'd have done anything to please his old man. Now, he tried his best to put him out of his mind.

"If there was anything here, the police have already found it." He moved closer, so close she stepped backward. His size was intimidating, his angry eyes scorching her. "Unless you know some place he might have kept things? Did he have a safe-deposit box? A secret safe somewhere?"

She shook her head. The rich timbre of his voice was so deep it was almost threatening. And titillating, as well.

Craig Horn was the kind of man who could battle the most ruthless of bastards. But he also could bring a woman to climax in record time.

She didn't know why that thought occurred to her, but she sensed it was true. And her body was tingling just looking at his big hands. Remembering the feel of them on her back, pressing her close, trying to protect her.

He stepped even closer, invading her space so she felt the hint of his breath on her cheek.

"Do you know something you aren't telling me?"

She shook her head, fighting the urge to run. Olivia Thornbird had never let a man intimidate her, but the Iceman's sexual prowess was almost more than she could bear.

"If you have information on the case, Olivia, you have to share it with me." He traced a finger down her shoulder, making her shiver. "You want me to find out what happened, don't you?"

She stiffened. He was purposely trying to throw her off balance. A tough, brooding, silent type now playing the comforting, caring man to siphon information. She knew the game. Had used it herself.

And he had his technique down pat.

But she couldn't fall into the trap.

"How do I know that you don't already have the answers?" she asked. "That you aren't keeping the truth from me?"

Touché. She could see it in his eyes. He'd planned to lie. "Is that what happened with your mother?"

She swallowed hard. She hadn't expected that tactic. "What do you know about her?"

He shrugged. "Just that she died while researching a virus years ago."

"Yes, and the government covered it up."

"You have proof of this?" Craig asked.

She hesitated, wishing she had. "No."

"Maybe your father wanted to protect you."

"Is that what you're doing, Agent Horn? Trying to protect me like you did my father?"

A muscle twitched in his jaw, a long silence stretching between them before he finally replied, "I'm sorry about your father, Olivia."

His gruff voice barely hinted at the emotions teetering to the surface. But he squared himself to his full height, ungiving. "I know you want to investigate," Craig said in a steely voice. "But this might be dangerous, Olivia. Stay out of it."

"I don't care if it is dangerous." She jutted up her chin. "I've lost everyone, Horn. The only thing I have to live for is to find out the reason why."

His eyes darkened, the silence so intense she could have sworn she felt the molecules of air colliding around her. Then his gaze dropped to her hand. She'd forgotten she was still holding the threatening note.

The paper crinkled between her fingers as he slid his hand over hers and pried it from her fingers.

Chapter Five

A tingle jolted Craig as he wrapped his fingers around Olivia's hand and lifted it. Her fingers were long, slender, her nails short but manicured. And her skin was so soft it felt like silk.

She clenched the note tightly, as if she didn't want him to see what she held. "What's this?"

She shrugged, acting nonplussed. "Nothing."

He wasn't going to fall for her innocent act. "Then you won't mind me taking a look."

It was more of a statement than a question. She tossed her head back—a reaction to the sound of his husky tone or simply stubborn bravado? His body twitched with arousal at the thought. In spite of being obstinate and determined, she was so damn sexy he was tempted to drag her in his arms and kiss her.

At the same time, he wanted to handcuff her to the inside of his car and keep her there so he could prevent her from causing more trouble. Or getting into it herself.

He did neither.

Her soft, warm hand contrasted sharply with the

unyielding resistance in her eyes. Then he unfolded the small scrap of paper and all teasing left his mind.

Dr. Thornbird, if you don't back off, you're dead.

His gaze shot to hers. "Where did you get this?"

She hesitated long enough to make him wonder if she would lie.

"In one of my father's lab coat pockets."

"I can't believe CSI missed that. And now your fingerprints are all over it."

This time, the defiance slipped at the contempt in his voice. But she recovered quickly. "It's proof that someone wanted to hurt my father."

"Evidence that you hadn't planned to give the police?" he growled.

She hesitated as if she meant to argue, then clamped her mouth shut.

"You have to work with me here, Olivia. How the hell can I solve the case if you withhold evidence?"

"How the hell do I know what you'll do with it?" Her voice exploded with anger and distrust. "For all I know, you're hiding information from me now. And when you find out the truth, you'll finagle a big government cover-up just like before."

"You said yourself you have no proof of a cover-up."

The pain that clouded her eyes tore at him. Chipped at the layers of ice.

"But I know it's true. Your father is a senator, Agent Horn. And you work for the feds. You're probably all in cahoots."

His temper flared, halting the thawing process. "If you're suggesting that my father is corrupt or that I can be bought, Miss Thornbird, you're wrong."

She shrugged, as if untouched by his harsh tone. "Then prove it. Work with me. Give me the story."

"So you can print speculations that will terrify the city and create panic?"

"Maybe people should be terrified. If they know the truth, then they can protect themselves."

He hesitated. He saw her point, but her theories were flawed. Panic would only compound the problem, hinder the investigation. And the crazies that would call in would only complicate things, occupy much needed, valuable manpower that would better be used in another capacity.

His past rose to haunt him. His father's ridiculing words. His stupidity in falling for another beautiful woman. A sexy reporter who'd used him…

He wasn't a young ignorant man any more. And he wouldn't fall for Olivia, no matter how much he wanted to soothe her pain.

No. Craig Horn was FBI. He couldn't make promises he might not be able to keep or let things get personal.

And he couldn't share anything with Olivia that she might put in print.

But what if she was right? What if he did discover a cover-up?

He dismissed the thought with the calculated ease of a seasoned agent. If he did, he'd deal with it like a professional. Weigh the costs. The benefits. Do what he had to do, just as he always did. The end justified the means. Emotions couldn't enter the picture. "I don't have to prove anything to you, Miss Thornbird."

"Spoken like a true agent. The Iceman, right?"

He fisted his hands by his sides, wondering why her comment irked him so. When others called him that, he swelled with pride. "That's what I am. Now, don't get in the way of my job."

Olivia's eyes flashed fire. "I'm doing what I have to do, too."

Apparently they'd reached a standoff. The sooner this case was solved, the sooner Olivia Thornbird would be out of his life. "Did you find something other than the note?"

She threaded her fingers through her hair, lifting it from her neck as if she was hot. Unfortunately, the movement only drew attention to the slender column of her throat and its satiny softness. He loosened his tie, perspiration beading his neck. The air conditioner must not be working.

"No, but I'd like to look around some more."

"Did your father have a safe-deposit box?"

"I told you, no."

He dragged his gaze from her hair, gestured toward the threatening note. "I'll have this analyzed."

She nodded, the tension between them vibrating with distrust and other emotions neither of them wanted to acknowledge. The memory of her father's last few moments filtered through the haze, connecting them.

But the questions about his death created a gulf that separated them.

Craig's guilt lay somewhere in the middle.

The pain in her eyes beckoned him to cross over. Their jobs, their beliefs, *her* need for vengeance stood as firm reminders that he couldn't.

FOR A BRIEF MINUTE, Olivia had almost allowed herself to believe that Craig Horn was human. That he was going to reach out and assuage her worries, offer to help her, to tell her everything.

But she knew better. He was just as cold as she'd heard.

The feds, the cops, the politicians—they were all alike. Sure, they did their jobs, and even put their lives on the line for others. But in the end, they protected their reputations no matter who got hurt in the process.

Just like those scientists at Nighthawk Island. Playing God. Conducting unethical experiments. Performing mind-altering games on that one cop. Killing one of their own scientists to keep their secrets.

She'd made attempts to get the scoop on the inner workings of CIRP for months, but so far had made little headway. Ian Hall appeared to be trying to change the image.

But an image was only what one saw on the surface. It was what lay beneath that intrigued her.

Just like Agent Craig Horn was beginning to intrigue her.

But she didn't want to be intrigued by him. Or attracted to him. And she especially didn't want to wonder what would happen if she could melt the ice around his heart.

"All right," Horn said, "let's look around."

His deep sexy voice pulled her from her thoughts. She glanced up and moved away from him, rattled. He was too close. Too intense. Too good at what he did—uncovering the truth.

And she had no intention of letting him see inside her, of knowing the real Olivia.

"I don't need help."

His harsh bark of laughter didn't surprise her.

"You don't need help with anything, do you, Olivia?"

She swallowed, wishing he wouldn't say her name in that husky timbre. Even without meaning to, it reverberated with sultry undertones that sent sensations skittering up her spine.

"I'd like some privacy, that's all." She gestured around her father's room, noted the fingerprint dust on the surfaces, and shuddered. "I deserve that, don't I?"

His quiet breath hissed through the air, adding to the steeping tension. "Yes. But we both know whatever you find might be useful to my investigation, so I don't intend to leave."

Anger churned through her. At him. At the circumstances.

But he was right, and she couldn't deny it.

Besides, two could play the game. He probably had connections to privileged information at CIRP. Maybe he'd slip up and reveal something.

Maybe *she* could use *him*.

"Okay." Ignoring the hint of a smile that indicated he thought he'd won this round, she turned away and searched her father's closet. The same few pairs of brown and black slacks that were nearly threadbare hung side by side with his white dress shirts that were equally as old, some with missing buttons and tattered collars, along with an overcoat he'd had since she was a child. The house shoes she'd given him ten years before lay on the floor, three pairs of socks rolled up beside them, another stack of medical journals in the corner.

She knelt to examine the back of the closet in hopes of finding a lockbox or something filled with notes, but found nothing. Behind her, Horn checked the night-stand, then pawed through the dresser. Irritated, she reached for the top shelf. Two hats, an umbrella, gloves and a pack of cigarettes. She ran her hand along the back of the shelf and discovered a photo album.

Her breath caught as she opened the book and saw the carefully inserted pictures. Her parents on their wedding day, looking happy and young and in love. The two of them on a jaunt to Asia. Then her mother pregnant. She ran her finger over her mother's face, affection welling in her throat. The next page held pictures of her as an infant, then cataloged her growth to a toddler. Her in her mother's arms. Her father giving her a bottle. Her mother carrying her in a backpack as they hiked into the mountains.

Odd, but she didn't remember many family outings. By the time she was five, both her parents had turned their focus back on their careers, as if their research were more important than her. She remembered cold TV dinners, late nights with a babysitter, phone calls from foreign countries.

And her mother's last trip—Egypt. She'd phoned saying she was coming home early. Olivia had been so excited, she'd taken markers and created a half-dozen Welcome Home posters. In a rare moment, her father had come home early, and they'd baked homemade chocolate cookies for dessert.

She swiped at a tear trickling down her cheek, the memory so real it felt as if it had just happened. And then the phone call. Her mother was never coming back.

Her father's anguished cry. His fury at the authorities for not answering his questions about her death. The sudden silence in the house when he'd walked out and left her alone to cry.

It was the last time she had allowed herself to. Until the day her father died.

"Olivia?"

Embarrassed, she closed the book and hugged it to her. "Did you find something?"

She shook her head. "No." The room suddenly seemed stifling. Her father's smell lingered in the air. His memory. It was choking her.

And the sympathetic look in Horn's eyes—she couldn't handle it.

He moved closer, the faint woodsy smell growing closer.

Unable to breathe or remain in the room any longer, she turned and fled, hugging the album to her. When she drove away seconds later, she didn't look back. Although she knew that Craig Horn had followed her outside, that he was watching her. That he'd started to say something to comfort her, but then he'd pulled back.

Because he was the cold man she'd always thought. And just like her father, he put his job first. He didn't have time for emotional entanglements.

And neither did she. Getting involved only meant getting hurt.

She'd already suffered enough pain and loneliness for a lifetime.

IN SPITE OF HIS VOW to harden himself against Olivia, Craig's chest squeezed as he watched her flee the house and drive away. Her sorrow had moved something inside him, something he hadn't felt for a long time. Maybe never.

He scrubbed a hand over his chin, banished the images, told himself she was part of a case, that was all. Nothing more.

Except she was persistent and would be back.

Her momentary escape had been a spontaneous reaction to the circumstances. She would beat herself up later for revealing those emotions.

He was beginning to understand her. She wasn't as tough as she wanted everyone to believe. And that tiny chink in her armor, that small vulnerability that had peeked through the mask, was getting to him.

His cell phone jangled and he grabbed it, grateful for the interruption. "Agent Horn."

"Horn, it's Adam Black from the Savannah Police Department."

God, he hoped they didn't have another victim so soon. "Yeah?"

"We've been searching the national database for similar cases to the suicides. We might be on to something."

"I'll be right over."

He hung up and headed toward the door. On the floor, he spotted a small photograph that must have fallen from the album when Olivia had run from the house. The picture showed a gap-toothed first-grade Olivia traipsing after her mother on a hiking trip. He frowned, those sad, big blue eyes yanking at his insides.

Her comments about her mother's death echoed in his head like a broken record. Ruth Thornbird had died of a strange virus in a foreign country.

And now her husband had died of one, too.

But Olivia's mother's death had occurred fifteen years ago. They couldn't possibly be related, could they?

FURIOUS WITH HERSELF for getting upset in front of Craig Horn, Olivia make a firm pact with herself that it wouldn't happen again. She was tough. Invincible. Going to do her job in spite of the barricades tossed in her path.

Desperate for answers, she decided to go to CIRP. Ian Hall had already proven to be a dead end. But if she could get into her father's office…

She swung back by the house to see if Agent Horn was still there, but he'd left, so she slipped back inside, borrowed one of her father's lab coats, found a clean scrub suit and pulled it on over her clothes. Then she found her father's name tag, coded with his entrance passkey, and stuffed it in her pocket. Hopefully, they hadn't disarmed his code yet.

The muggy heat was stifling as she headed toward the research park, the scents of salt water and fish swirling through her car windows as she drove along the shore. Perspiration dotted her neck where she'd twisted her hair into a knot beneath the surgical cap. Confident she could pull off the disguise as an employee, she parked and climbed the steps to the research building where her father had worked. She scanned the area, went through the front door, then waited until a group of med techs filed through security to mingle with the crowd. Thankfully, she passed through unnoticed. Grateful she had visited her father at his office, she understood the layout of the building, knew she'd need the passkey on the third floor before entering the wing to his office. Two doctors were conferring in the hall near the security lock, so she ducked behind the corner until they left, then hurried forward, swiped the key and waited for the lock to be released.

Seconds later, she was in her father's office. The scent of chemicals floated through the sterile atmosphere, the various test tubes and machinery familiar although she'd never actually paid attention to her father's ramblings about their functions.

Now she wished she'd listened more carefully.

Her nerves fluttered at the sound of voices outside the door. She stooped lower, then slid into the desk chair, waiting until they passed by. Finally clear, she booted up her father's computer and tried to access his recent files.

When she scrolled down the menu, she noticed a file marked Ruth Thornbird. Her heart fluttered. She clicked on the file, tapping her toe while she waited. Seconds later, just as the information began to appear on the screen, the door opened behind her.

"What are you doing in here?"

She had just enough time to glance at the screen, to see the name Dr. Martin Shubert, before the guards yanked her out of the chair and dragged her down the hall.

CRAIG SHOOK HANDS WITH Detective Adam Black and claimed the seat across the desk from him. His partner, Clayton Fox, spread several computer printouts on the table.

"What did you find?" Craig asked.

"We've been investigating CIRP for some time now," Detective Black began.

Horn nodded, then turned to Clayton Fox. "I know

that they altered your memory to make you think you were someone else for a while in order to throw you off your investigation."

"Yes, it was quite an ordeal," Fox said. "But thankfully, I'm back to normal."

"I understand you think each of the suicide victims contracted a virus," Detective Black said.

Horn nodded. "We're trying to learn more about it now."

"What if the virus has nothing to do with the suicides?" Black asked.

Horn shrugged. "It's possible. Right now, we're playing a hunch. We did consider the possibility of a cult, but haven't found any connections to the victims and any cults." He gestured toward the files. "What are you thinking?"

"That perhaps the victims were brainwashed, maybe hypnotized."

"Given a hypnotic suggestion to commit suicide?" Horn chewed the inside of his cheek. "That's possible, I suppose. But I didn't think people could be given suggestions that would make them do things against their natural will?"

Black frowned. "I already spoke with a therapist about it. She said if the patient were drugged, it might be possible."

"After what they did to me," Detective Fox said, "I believe anything is possible."

"But the victims would have to have a connection to the same therapist, right?"

"The first two victims did see a therapist, a Dr. Janine Woodward."

"Let me guess," Horn said. "She works for CIRP."

The detectives both smiled, confirming his assumption. Horn stood. "Good work, Detectives. I say we pay Dr. Woodward a visit."

"MISS THORNBIRD, WE DON'T appreciate you trying to break into confidential files."

"They belonged to my father," Olivia argued. "I have a right to see them."

Ian Hall's accusatory look scalded her. "Not when they pertain to restricted projects that are government classified."

"I thought you wanted to cooperate with the police," Olivia argued, "and help find out what's causing this virus."

"I am cooperating with the police, but you are not one of them. You're a reporter digging for a story."

"I'm one of the victims' daughters searching for the truth." Furious, she snatched her purse from the guard and headed toward the door. Another security guard stepped in front of her, barring the exit with his massive body. A third guard approached her from the side, his size towering over her at least three inches, his weight at least a hundred pounds more than her own.

"Miss Thornbird, don't come back here," Ian Hall warned. "If you do, I'll have you arrested."

She planted her hands on her hips. "And if I find out that you've hidden something about this virus, something that poses a danger to the public, or that you're responsible for the virus here at CIRP, I'll see that the story is printed, even if it's from my deathbed."

"Be careful with your threats, Miss Thornbird. You might wind up eating your words."

Olivia gave him a last menacing look, then bolted past the guards and out the door. The trembles started as soon as she settled in her car, but she fought them. She wouldn't let Ian Hall or anyone else deter her. Somehow, she'd find a way to breach the security and unlock the truth about what was going on here at CIRP and why her father had died. And if they knew anything about her mother...

Deciding to go home and check her computer for the name she'd seen on her father's screen, she swung a sharp right, hit the gas pedal and drove to her apartment. Dark storm clouds threatened above, the sound of thunder rumbling in the sky. Lightning zigzagged above the live oaks, the muggy heat engulfing her as she parked in front of her apartment.

Still shaky, she climbed out, frowning when she noticed her front door ajar. Someone had been inside. Remembering the threatening phone call she'd received earlier, she hesitated, grabbed her cell phone from her purse and slowly walked up the cobblestoned steps. Her fingers poised to punch 911, she peered inside.

Behind her, more thunder cracked. No, it was a gunshot.

The bullet pierced her shoulder, and she bounced backward, pain searing through her. A second bullet pinged off the front door, and she screamed, then ducked and dropped to the ground. Blood gushed from the wound and dripped onto her hands as she crawled to the bushes to hide.

Chapter Six

Craig and the detectives were walking out the door when one of the uniforms caught Detective Black's arm.

"Nine-one-one just came in from Olivia Thornbird's home address. Thought you might want to know."

Craig stiffened. "What's wrong?"

"She's been shot. Someone broke into her house. That's all we've got."

Craig's vision momentarily blanked as the blood rushed to his head.

Detective Black directed a clipped nod toward the other officer. "Has anyone else responded yet?"

"Officers Morley and Batterson were close by. They're there now."

"Come on, Horn." Black picked up the pace. "You can ride with us."

Craig and the detectives rushed to the police car, Craig's mind racing as Black flipped on the siren and sped through town. Images of Olivia, bloody and dying, flashed through his head. Then another image appeared—the attacker waiting for her when she'd arrived home, ambushing her, gunning her down in cold blood.

The Savannah squares and graveyard whirled past. Concrete tombstones and monuments stood in rows, the symbols of death macabre in the murky gray light. The fear that Olivia might be severely injured, that she might be joining her father in the grave twisted his insides.

He had told Olivia that he'd take care of things. Had promised to protect the citizens.

But he'd failed. Her father had died. And now someone had tried to kill her.

It seemed like an eternity, but Black finally reached her street, the tires squealing as he parked. The two uniforms were already on the scene, their weapons drawn as well.

Craig scanned the area for the perp as he climbed from the vehicle. An elderly couple huddled together on the front porch of a neighboring house, their faces strained, while another couple pushing a baby stroller hurried from the area toward a van parked in a metered spot on the street.

As soon as he reached the stoop, he saw Olivia lying on the ground near the flower bed. Blood soaked her blouse and her face was milky white.

"The ambulance is on the way," one of the officers said.

"Anything on the shooter?" Craig asked.

"Gone when we arrived. Batterson's searching the inside now."

"Canvass the neighborhood," Detective Black ordered.

Officer Morley nodded and headed to the neighboring apartments and houses.

"Olivia." She was unconscious. Craig's throat jammed as he knelt and checked her pulse. It was weak and thready, but she was alive, although she had lost so much blood. "Olivia, can you hear me?"

Detective Fox retrieved a towel from the apartment and stuffed it in his hand. Craig tore open Olivia's blouse, the sight of the bullet wound piercing her shoulder wrenching his stomach. But at least the bullet had missed her heart. An inch or two lower…

He couldn't think about that now. He positioned her head into his lap, then pressed the towel firmly to the wound to stem the blood flow, applying pressure. A siren wailed in the distance, the ambulance zooming toward the house. Rain drizzled from the dark clouds, thunder rumbling louder, nearby. He lifted Olivia in his arms, cradled her under the umbrella of his body as he rushed toward the ambulance.

She moaned and clutched at his shirt, knotting the fabric in her hands. "Horn."

He leaned closer, rain drenching his clothes, droplets sliding off his chin. "Yeah, I've got you."

Her breath rattled out, unsteady and low. "Didn't mean to pass out."

A soft laugh escaped him. He should have known the stubborn woman would be mad at herself for showing any weakness.

"It's all right," he said gently. "I don't like blood myself." In fact, seeing her so faint made him feel weak-kneed, although he didn't understand why; he'd certainly seen much more severe injuries.

She reached up. Brushed at the moisture on his cheek. "S…sorry."

His throat tightened at her unexpected tenderness. The woman had been shot and she was apologizing for keeping him in the rain. "It's just water," he said in a gruff voice. "I'll survive."

The EMT and paramedic jumped from the ambulance. One opened the back, and they reached for the stretcher. Craig eased Olivia onto it, keeping the pressure firm on her injury as he dried her forehead with his handkerchief.

Her eyes fluttered open, the ghost of fear haunting her eyes.

"You're going to be all right," he whispered.

Black rushed up behind him. "Go with her. We'll let you know what we find here."

He nodded, then jumped into the back of the ambulance. The paramedic hooked Olivia up to an IV while the paramedic took her vitals and radioed them in to the hospital. Seconds later, the EMT fired up the engine and sped toward the hospital.

Rain poured down, fat droplets slashing the metal and pinging off the ambulance roof. He gathered Olivia's hand in his, rubbing her icy skin. "Did you see the shooter?"

She shook her head, licked her parched lips. "No. From behind." Her eyes fluttered closed, her lower lip quivering. "Please…don't…go," she whispered.

The sound of the wailing siren nearly drowned out her request.

Or maybe it was the roaring of his own blood in his ears at the thought that she might have died.

"I'm right here," he said hoarsely.

She nodded, giving into unconsciousness. His jaw hardened, emotions he didn't understand welling in his throat. The guilt he expected. The knot of fear he couldn't handle.

He shouldn't care what happened to the damn

woman. She was obstinate. Nosy. Had probably put herself in jeopardy by investigating her father's death. And when she awakened, she probably wouldn't remember asking him to stay with her. Hell, even if she did, she wouldn't admit it.

But still, he couldn't tear himself away from her side as they whirled into the hospital and the EMTs rushed her to the E.R. A few minutes later, after they took her to surgery, he paced the waiting room. She'd been hit pretty bad. But she was going to be all right.

So why couldn't he shake this feeling that something worse was going to happen? That even here in the hospital, Olivia wouldn't be safe, that he had to watch her every minute or someone might kill her as they had her father?

SHE WAS ALL ALONE. Again.

"Mommy, please don't leave me. Please come back...."

Her head spun as she reached for her mother's hand, but her fingers connected with thin air. Tears blurred her eyes and streamed down her cheeks. The smell of her mother's perfume lingered in the air like the lilacs she used to grow out back. But the flowers had all died; they'd turned brown because her mother hadn't been there to water them.

"Mommy, please," she cried, "the lilacs are dying. I miss you...."

"Hush now, Livvy," her father said. "Mommy's never coming back. Don't act like a baby."

"I'm not a baby." She lashed out at her father with her fists, but he gripped her hands, picked her up and placed her on her bed in the corner of the dark room,

then stalked away. Thunder rumbled. Rain slashed the window, rattling the house. It was scary outside.

Then he was gone. And she was alone in the dark.

She rocked herself back and forth on her bed, clutching the covers around her. "Please don't leave, I don't want to be alone..."

"I'm here, Olivia."

The voice...it didn't belong to her father. Or her mother. But who was there?

She struggled to open her eyes, but they were so heavy, her limbs felt weighted. Her arm ached, too, and her mouth was so dry.

"Rest now. I'll be here when you wake up."

The deep husky voice reverberated through the darkness. Filled the claustrophobic air. Then something warm touched her hand. Fingers closed around hers, stroked her palm gently.

Her breathing steadied. Then she was alone again.

A dizzy feeling swept her into a vortex of darkness. Pain knifed through her. The world spun, and she was falling into the unknown.

And no one was there to catch her.

EVEN AS CRAIG HELD Olivia's hand in the recovery room and assured her that he wouldn't let anything happen to her, fear gripped him. He'd failed his sister. Her father.

What if he failed her?

She looked impossibly small and vulnerable in the hospital bed with the bandage around her shoulder. The harsh overhead lights accentuated her pale face, the listless sound of her breathing troubling him.

The nurse frowned. "There's a detective asking for you in the waiting room."

"I'll be back, Olivia." He squeezed her hand one more time, then slipped from the room and met Black in the hall.

"How is she?" Detective Black asked.

"She'll make it. Bullet missed her heart and lungs."

"Did she get a look at the shooter?"

Craig shook his head. "He came at her from behind. What did you find in her apartment?"

"Someone trashed the place," Black said. "Her computer files are destroyed."

"He was looking for something." Craig shook his head grimly. "Probably trying to find out what she knew about her father's death."

"Hell, she's a reporter," Black said. "We don't know for sure that the break-in and assault had anything to do with her dad or the suicide cases. It could have been another story."

It could be, but that was doubtful. "I'll check with her when she wakes up. See what else she was working on." Craig rammed his hand through his hair. "Get any fingerprints at her place?"

"We've dusted and are running them now. You still want to question that psychologist?"

He nodded. "Yes, but I'd like to leave a guard at Olivia's door."

"I'll arrange for a uniform to watch her."

A few minutes later, Craig left a heavyset officer named O'Malley standing guard beside the recovery room, while he and Black drove to CIRP. They met with Ian Hall first.

Hall's eyebrows rose when Craig relayed the latest turn of events. "Olivia Thornbird was shot?"

"Yes." Craig studied the man's cool facade. "You didn't know?"

"How the hell would I?" Hall plucked at his tie. "Listen, Agent Horn, I told you I was trying to turn the publicity about the research park around and I am. What can I do for you?"

Craig still didn't know whether to believe him. "We want to speak to Dr. Woodward."

Hall immediately phoned her extension, then showed them to her office. Janine Woodward was tall, thin and elegant, with dark hair tucked neatly into a French twist, sensible shoes and green eyes that raked over each of them as if she were mentally assessing them. He supposed it was her nature, just like it was his job to do the same.

"Hello, gentlemen, what can I do for you?"

Craig didn't waste time. He explained their theories regarding the Savannah Suicides. "Two of the victims were your patients."

She stared at him dead-on, her reaction schooled. "I only saw them briefly, but was very sorry to hear about their suicides. I…wish I could have done more."

"We currently have some of your doctors and the CDC testing tissue samples to pinpoint the nature of the virus, cause and cure," Horn explained. "We're not convinced these were suicides."

Her eyes narrowed. "I don't understand. Each of the victims exhibited paranoia to the point of agoraphobia. I admit it was odd, but their behaviors were characteristic of suicide victims. I encouraged them to commit to in-patient therapy so I could monitor each of them, but both refused."

Black cut in, "We're aware that some of your mental health professionals have experimented with altering memories using a combination of drug therapy and hypnosis."

She crossed her legs and leaned back in her chair, appearing relaxed, but Horn could read people, too. She knew where he was heading, and she was nervous. "You and Clayton Fox were partners," she said. "I remember reading about you in the paper."

"Were you on the team who drugged him?" Black asked.

"No." She shifted, her thin lips tightening. "I only recently transferred to CIRP. Dr. Hall brought me in. I work with schizophrenics."

"Is it possible that you could give someone a post-hypnotic suggestion to commit suicide when they're in a psychotic or drug-induced state, and that the patient would follow through?"

She frowned. "I suppose it's possible, but highly unlikely. Although I was not involved in the experiment with Clayton Fox, I believe he proved that the subconscious mind is strong. He overcame the suggestions."

"But it is possible?" Horn pressed.

"Under certain circumstances, perhaps." She rose, folded her arms. "But I can assure you, gentlemen, that no one in my department, especially myself, would indulge in any treatment that's unethical. What purpose would it serve?"

Horn and Black traded skeptical looks. "I don't know," Craig said. "But if that's the case, we'll find out. And we'll be back to see you when we do."

OLIVIA DRIFTED IN AND OUT of consciousness, her nightmares bouncing between her mother's death, her father's suicide and the drug-induced hallucinations caused by the medication. She should have warned the doctors she couldn't handle narcotics.

The hazy face of a doctor garbed in surgical clothes and mask drifted in front of her face, and she squinted. He had a small dark mole on his chin, and he smelled like disinfectant. She thought the surgery was over. That she was in recovery.

Then something pricked her arm. Another needle.

"No…" She tried to speak but her voice faded as the drugs seeped though her system. Then suddenly the bed shifted. Someone was moving her.

The face appeared again. No, not a face, only eyes peering at her over the surgical mask. Dark. Black. Empty.

A doctor?

The gurney hit a bump, a sea of blinding white drifting past as he rolled her into the hall. Dizziness swept her into a blur, and she decided he must be taking her to her room.

Maybe Craig Horn would come and visit.

Craig—he'd carried her to the ambulance. And he hadn't been cold. He'd held her hand on the way to the hospital. His voice had been so soothing.

She closed her eyes, allowing the memory to float with her and alleviate her panic as she drifted into unconsciousness again.

But a few minutes later, she roused, dizzy and slightly nauseated. Where was she?

She struggled to make out the room, but colors and lights swirled around her in a blinding fog. And she couldn't move.

A jolt of panic shot through her. She was paralyzed.

She tried to open her eyes, to cry out for help, but her vocal cords had shut down. The room was ice-cold. Pitch-black.

A man's voice broke the quiet, "Goodbye, Miss Thornbird."

The throaty voice reverberated with evil, stirring a memory from the past. The threatening phone calls...

A strangled sound erupted from her as realization dawned.

The man wasn't a doctor.

He slowly dragged a sheet over her legs, her torso, then draped it over her face, shutting out the light. She gasped for air, but she couldn't breathe.

Footsteps clicked on the hard floor. Hushed voices echoed in the background. Something about paperwork. Being processed.

"The Savannah Funeral Home will be over to pick up her body soon."

The words rang in her ears, sending horror through her. She was in the morgue. The drug the man had given her was going to kill her....

Then the voices faded and the door slammed shut, leaving her all alone. The darkness swallowed her, an odd tingling traveling down her spine and legs until numbness replaced the needle-like sensations.

Seconds later, the sensation that she was floating from her body followed.

She was going to die.

Craig's face materialized in her mind, sorrow filling her. She'd never get to see him again, never get to touch him or tell him goodbye....

Chapter Seven

Craig's cell phone trilled as he and Detective Black drove away from Catcall Island, the heart of CIRP's main facility. "Special Agent Horn."

"Agent Horn," the man stammered in a decidedly worried voice, "it's Officer O'Malley."

Craig's hand tightened around the handset. "What's wrong?"

"Listen...I hate to tell you this, but Miss Thornbird...well—"

"Spit it out, O'Malley."

"She's missing."

Craig ground his molars. "What do you mean, *missing?*"

"Well, the doctors and nurses, they've been in and out, and one of 'em said he was taking her to her room—" he paused, wheezing as if he'd been running, then continued "—so I stopped in the john, but when I came out and went to find her, she wasn't there."

An expletive tore from his mouth. "Black, step on it. Your damn officer lost Olivia."

Detective Black's expression turned ominous as

he cut into traffic, hit the siren and raced toward Savannah.

"Listen, O'Malley," Craig snapped, "get security to block all exits from the hospital. Issue a hospital alert for anyone who might be trying to kidnap Olivia, and do it now! We'll be there in five!"

"What the hell happened?" Detective Black asked when Craig disconnected.

Craig explained, then exploded, his imagination taking a wild ride. He'd been in law enforcement a damn long time, had seen gruesome things, almost as gruesome as in the military. "What kind of incompetent officers do you have working for you?"

Black maneuvered around a garbage truck. "Officer O'Malley's a good guy. Has three kids. If he lost this woman, he didn't do it intentionally."

"I told him to stay with her." Craig clenched the console with a white-knuckled grip. "If she dies, it's my fault."

Black steered around a Mustang and then cut across a sidestreet, the car bouncing as it hit a pothole. "It sounds like you really care about this woman."

If anything else happened to Olivia, he'd never forgive himself. "I just feel responsible," he said through gritted teeth. "If it wasn't for me, her father wouldn't have been investigating this virus."

"And his death dragged Olivia into it?"

Craig nodded.

"She's a reporter, Horn. She would have come after the story anyway."

He was right. But that did nothing to alleviate the guilt prickling Craig's conscience.

The rest of the ride was silent, fraught with apprehension, and when Black finally parked in front of the hospital, Craig jumped out. Straightening his suit coat, he ordered himself to bottle his emotions as he jogged into the hospital. Olivia Thornbird meant nothing to him. He was simply doing his job. But the image of her at the hands of a ruthless killer hacked at more than his conscience.

Officer O'Malley met him near the recovery room, the surgeon and head nurse beside him, both looking frantic.

"Did you find her?" Craig asked.

The nurse threw up her hands, her cheeks ballooning out. "I…don't understand what happened. I only left for a second to check on another patient."

"She was fine after surgery," Dr. Elgin said, his own pallor off. "We're checking all floors to see if she might have been moved to another room by mistake, and I have a guard checking the security tapes."

All of which would take time. Precious time that might cost Olivia her life.

Craig tried desperately to silence his internal panic button and set to work, issuing commands and coordinating the search for best efficiency. Mass confusion reigned for the next half hour. Craig, Black and O'Malley searched the hospital, coordinating with the security guard and another police team that had arrived after O'Malley's call. O'Malley had practically fallen all over himself apologizing, but Craig told him to save it for Olivia.

If they found her. He couldn't say it aloud.

Finally, the men gathered in the lobby to regroup. "We've checked all the exits and radioed all the ambulance drivers," one of the security guards said.

"So far, we haven't found any misplaced patients," another guard added.

Detective Black shuffled, a strained look on his face. "She couldn't have just disappeared into thin air."

"If you wanted to hide a body in a hospital, where would you do it?" Craig asked, struggling to remain rational when his own mind raced with the sickening possibilities.

"O.R.?" a nurse suggested.

"A storage room? Lab?" others offered.

"Get on it." Craig's stomach knotted as he considered another daunting possibility. If the kidnapper had already killed Olivia, the most logical place to stash her would be with the other deceased patients. "I'm going to check the morgue. Where is it?"

The guard pointed to the hall. "Cold room's in the basement."

O'Malley rushed to check the operating rooms, the guards took the labs, Detective Black hurried to make sure the nurses on each floor had verified patients' identities in case someone had switched charts and ID bracelets, and another guard reviewed the security tapes. Craig sprinted toward the elevator, jumped inside and punched the button for the basement.

The minute the elevator dinged and he stepped off, the atmosphere changed. The hall was dark, chilly, reeked of fetid odors. The scents of death wafted around him, the sound of metal clinking against steel echoing in the distance.

His pulse quickened as he read the signs and found the cold room.

A heavyset young man with square glasses held up

a hand. "Are you from the funeral home or coroner's office?"

Craig flipped open his identification. "Neither. Special Agent Craig Horn. I'm looking for a missing patient."

Cammy, an African-American woman wearing a nurse's uniform, frowned. "Name please?"

"Olivia Thornbird." He exhaled to control his agitation. "But I need to check all the patients. It's possible someone switched her ID bracelet."

The orderly and nurse traded skeptical looks, then gestured for him to follow Cammy into the refrigerated room. A chill slid down his spine at the sight of the sheet-draped bodies. One of them might be Olivia.

Hell, what was wrong with him? He'd seen dead bodies over the years, but never felt the mind-boggling fear that gripped him as he imagined Olivia under one of those sheets.

Cammy stopped by the first steel table and read the toe tag, then checked it against her chart. His breath caught as she lifted the sheet, then gushed out when he saw an Asian woman's battered naked body on the gurney.

"It's not her." Regret for the woman mingled with relief that it hadn't been Olivia. Then they quickly moved on to the next gurney and the next, each time, his breathing growing more difficult, the sweat pouring down his neck and back.

By the time they reached the third row, the scent of death, body odors and chemicals had made him nauseous, and his hands shook violently as he reached for the sheet.

He muttered a silent prayer as he lifted it, his lungs fighting for oxygen.

Her blond hair lay in tangles, her cheeks pale and bloodless. "Olivia."

He gasped her name, then touched her hand. It was limp. And she lay so still, as in death. His pulse accelerated as he reached for her wrist to check her pulse.

But he couldn't find one.

"DID YOU TAKE CARE OF the Thornbird woman?"

The streetlights nearly blinded him as he exited the hospital parking lot. He gripped the phone, steered his sedan onto the street and grinned. Apparently the two men in charge had disagreed on how to handle Miss Thornbird. Milaski wanted the woman to print the story. But the master thought it was a dicey move, one that would draw too much attention. "Yeah. She shouldn't give you any more problems."

The man on the other end of the line wheezed in relief. "I wish it hadn't come to this."

Although it was hot as Hades outside, he imagined his boss leaning back in his expensive leather chair, pressing a hand over the silk lining of his smoking jacket, lighting up a Cuban cigar, looking cool as a cucumber in his air-conditioned office with its plush furniture, imported oriental rugs and crystal decanters of bourbon and scotch.

His grin broadened. The man acted tough, but he was scared of his own shadow, afraid of exposing himself. Thought his own hands and those manicured nails too precious and important to dirty.

But those hands *had* done dirty things before, things that to him were unimaginable.

"You covered your tracks?" his boss finally said.

He rolled his eyes. "Of course. Now you can get on with business."

"But her death may draw out all those maggots at the newspaper, as well as the cops."

"The Savannah Suicides story wasn't the only one she was working on."

"Yeah, but her father just died. People will assume—"

He chuckled. "You know what they say about people who assume—they're as—"

"This isn't funny." In spite of his polish, his boss's voice echoed with anxiety. "There are things the feds can't know."

"Don't sweat it. When they look at Olivia Thornbird's files, they'll see that she had enemies."

A sigh of relief echoed back. "Good plan."

He gritted his teeth. He had a brain, he wasn't just muscle like his boss thought. One day, maybe he'd figure that out.

A police car cruised by, and he checked his speed, not wanting to draw attention to himself. The freaking hospital had been swarming with cops. And that federal officer. Horn.

He was a problem.

But he could be taken care of, too. Although killing cops and FBI agents was chancy. But he'd do what had to be done. What he'd been trained to do.

Because he was a born killer.

OLIVIA HAD THE ODDEST sensation of leaving her body. There was a bright light. A light so strong she felt compelled to drift toward it. A hazy white encircled her like *a cloud of soft angel wings, the air tingling with a peaceful feeling that left her weightless and calm.*

Through the haze, a face appeared. A smile. The whisper of a voice.

Her mother's. So soft. Warm. Loving.

She reached out, almost touched her hand. But her fingers slipped.

Her mother shook her head. "Go back, Livvy. It's not your time."

A gut-wrenching sadness engulfed her. "No…please don't leave me again, Mom…"

"Later…" Her mother's voice faded, then she sailed farther away.

"OLIVIA, COME BACK to me," a male voice said. "Come on, you can do it."

Something hard pressed against Olivia's chest. Intense pressure. Voices bobbed through the fog, growing louder. Closer.

An electric jolt shot through her. Her body jerked.

"Again," a female voice ordered. "One-two-three." Another jolt. Her body bounced upward. A beeping sound intruded in the quiet.

"We've got a pulse!" someone shouted.

"She's alive!"

"Thank God!" another voice murmured.

A man's. One she recognized. Craig Horn's.

The bright light faded completely. Reality returned as she struggled to open her eyes. More bright lights, but this time they blinded her.

"Olivia, it's Craig. You're going to be all right."

Her memory rushed back. The man moving her. The fatal injection. The morgue.

Craig Horn had saved her life.

CRAIG REFUSED TO LEAVE Olivia's side the rest of the night. If it had taken him five minutes longer to find her, Olivia would have been dead.

Detective Black tapped on the door and stepped into the room. "How's she doing?"

Craig balled his hands into fists. She was still too damn pale. Had barely managed to open her eyes twice. And she looked as weak as a kitten. "She's alive. No thanks to the Savannah Police Department."

Black shook his head, obviously frustrated as well. "O'Malley worked with a sketch artist, but the man who moved Olivia was disguised in scrubs, complete with mask and cap, so there's not much to go on."

Craig nodded. "She was injected with a potassium solution which causes heart failure."

"So it's possible our perp has some kind of medical background, at least a minimal knowledge."

"With the Internet, all it takes these days is a little surfing. As long as he can read, any moron with access to a computer can commit murder."

"We've questioned the staff," Detective Black said. "But so far, no one seems suspicious."

"Could have been a doctor from CIRP."

Black nodded. "Listen, my wife's expecting. I'm going home for the night. Call me if there are any new developments."

Craig mumbled agreement. Agitated over the lack of

progress in the investigation, he checked his cell phone messages but had nothing from Agent Devlin. A message from his father surprised him.

"What in the hell is the FBI doing to solve this Savannah suicide streak, Craig?" his father bellowed into the phone. "Word is that the deaths may be related to terrorism. Is that true? With the senatorial election next year and germ warfare a hot topic on the political agenda, I need you to make this thing go away quietly. Call me ASAP."

Craig shook his head, furious. As usual, his father was more concerned about his political position than about Craig or the lives of citizens.

Olivia stirred, and he scooted closer to her bed, disturbed over his feelings. For the Iceman, this woman was certainly getting to him. Melting his defenses.

Hell, he might disagree with her about printing the truth about the virus, but at least her intentions were motivated by a will to help the public. Even Oberman, the head of the DPS, wanted to keep things quiet, not only to stem panic, but to guard his own reputation.

A low moan reverberated from Olivia, then her eyes fluttered open. They appeared glassy, her pupils slightly dilated, a confused look pulling at her mouth. "Craig?"

"Yeah, I'm here."

She blinked as if he was out of focus. "You…you saved my life."

His jaw tightened. Hell, he'd almost let her get killed. Those long agonizing minutes in the morgue rushed back. The smells, the feel of her stiff, cold hands… He shuddered. "You're going to be all right."

She licked her lips, so he held a cup of water to her mouth and let her sip slowly.

"Thank…you." She clenched the sheet between her fingers. "What happened?"

"A man disguised as a doctor slipped into the recovery room, injected you with a drug to cause a heart attack, then hid you downstairs."

"Oh, God, yes." Fear darkened her eyes. "I…remember. He took me there and left me."

"Did you see his face?"

She shook her head, her eyes flaring with terror.

"Did he say anything, Olivia?"

"Just good…goodbye."

His jaw tightened. "We'll find him."

She forced a small smile, although she winced immediately as if even that small movement hurt.

He cleared his throat, forcing himself to regain control, to think like an FBI agent. "What happened earlier today, before you were shot?"

Her eyes narrowed. "Went…went to CIRP. Tried to look at my father's files."

"Did you find anything?"

"Got caught." Her breath rattled out. "Guards took me to Dr. Hall."

He leaned his elbows on his knees. "Let me guess, he wasn't very happy to see you."

"Threatened to arrest me if I came back," she said in a strained voice.

He grimaced. Hall knew Olivia well enough to realize she wouldn't give up.

Had he sent someone after her to frighten her from

looking further into her father's death? Or had someone else at CIRP found out she'd been snooping around? Someone with secrets to hide?

Someone who would kill to protect his work?

Chapter Eight

Olivia had nightmares of the morgue all night.

Dead bodies lay next to her, staring at her with wide-open eyes. The room was ice-cold. She couldn't move. Then she levitated from her body toward the bright light.

The funeral home had come for her. She could see the mortician waiting with his instruments, smell the stench of embalming fluid...see her own casket waiting.

She jerked awake, trembling, her arm throbbing. The IV tugged at her skin as she rolled over and scanned the sterile hospital room.

Craig Horn was slumped over in the chair beside her bed. He hadn't left her side all night.

A wave of tenderness washed over her. In sleep, he still seemed tortured, aloof, but he also looked impossibly handsome and sexy in his rumpled gray suit and tie. His long legs were sprawled in front of a muscular body that she imagined in tight-fitting jeans and a T-shirt that would emphasize his impressive physique. The dark stubble on his cheeks beckoned her to touch him, the wide jaw that was normally set with determination and anger was slack, his chest rising and falling with steady, even breaths.

She remembered him holding her hand the night before, pulling her from the dark abyss of death, soothing her when she'd known she was going to die.

His eyes slowly fluttered open, and his gaze met hers. Steady. Probing. Icy? No… "How do you feel?"

She battled for a smile and lost. "A little sore. But I'll be all right."

"Tough Olivia." His husky voice skated over raw nerve endings that needed his gentle touch again this morning. A strained heartbeat of silence stretched between them as she remembered pleading with him not to leave her.

"I don't think I was very tough last night."

A small smile quirked at the corner of his mouth. "A lesser person would have given up and died."

She almost had. If it hadn't been for him…

The nurse pushed inside with a cart and took Olivia's vitals. Craig moved aside to the window, offering her a semblance of privacy as the nurse redressed her wound, but at the same time Olivia felt his presence, his eyes watching her as if he didn't trust the staff.

On the heels of the nurse's visit, the surgeon sauntered in, Olivia's chart in his hand. He pushed wire-rimmed glasses up on his nose and smiled. "You look considerably better this morning."

"I am," Olivia said. The nurse propped a pillow behind her to help her sit at an angle, then handed her a pill and left.

"Your vitals look good," the doctor said. "You should be able to go home in a couple of days."

"A couple of days?" Olivia asked.

"You need to rest," Dr. Elgin said. "You've had surgery and a near heart attack."

"But I can't stay here," Olivia protested. "I need to go home. I have things to do."

Craig cleared his throat. "Olivia—"

"No." Olivia swung her legs to the side. The movement sent her into a dizzy spell, but she gripped the sides of the bed to steady herself and concentrated on bringing the beige linoleum floor squares into focus. "Really, I'll rest better at home. Please…I can't stay here. I… hate hospitals."

Craig and the doctor exchanged concerned looks. "No one enjoys them," Dr. Elgin said, "but we're liable for your health, Miss Thornbird."

Olivia glanced at the IV. "If you're worried about a lawsuit, don't be."

"Olivia, please, let them take care of you," Craig said.

She gave him an imploring look. "I… Don't make me stay here, Craig. Please. Every time I close my eyes I see that morgue."

Craig swallowed, and she prayed she'd made her point.

Dr. Elgin tapped his pen on the chart. "Do you have family at home to take care of you?"

Olivia felt her face pale a deeper white, but Craig stepped forward. "Don't worry, Dr. Elgin, Olivia won't be left alone."

Olivia stiffened. Craig Horn might have saved her life, but she didn't intend to let him order her around or watch her as if she needed a caretaker.

"And besides, she's right," Craig said in a derisive tone. "We already know that the safest place for Olivia isn't here."

The doctor looked apologetic, but Olivia gulped at the thought of Craig invading her personal space.

Spending the night in her apartment. Filling it with his presence and his smell and his intimidating size.

But she couldn't work at all in the hospital, and she had to research the name she'd read in her father's files.

"Let me check your latest blood and urine samples to make certain the potassium isn't still in your system. Then we'll talk."

Olivia forced herself to lie back and rest for a few minutes while the doctor left to check on the lab results. Craig remained silent, his steely gaze shooting from her to the window as if he wasn't quite sure what to say.

A few strained minutes later, the doctor finally returned. "Your tests look good," he said, then reluctantly signed off on her release. "But I want to see you back in a few days to remove those stitches and recheck the wound. Now stay put, Miss Thornbird. A nurse will bring a wheelchair to escort you to the car."

She opened her mouth to argue, but he cut her off. "Hospital policy."

A nervous energy hummed between them as the doctor left. Finally, Craig turned to her, his mask in place, his somber look revealing nothing. "Listen, I know you're going to protest, Olivia, but we have to find a way to work together."

Shock fluttered through her. "You want to work with me?"

He gave a clipped nod, meaning he didn't, but he had no choice. "If you agree not to print anything about the virus investigation until we've concluded the investigation and solved the case, I'll give you an exclusive on the story."

She hesitated, then agreed. She'd find out more if she worked with him than she would on her own. Besides, someone had tried to kill her. She'd be a fool not to accept his help.

But could she trust him to keep his word? When the case ended, would he try to cover up the truth as the government had before?

CRAIG HAD NO IDEA when he'd made the decision to designate himself as Olivia's bodyguard, but he damn sure didn't trust anyone else right now and he had to keep her alive.

While she dressed, he phoned for a police car to drive them home. She seemed exceptionally quiet while the nurse wheeled her out to the car, even refusing his outstretched hand and offer of help. She had grit, he had to give her that, although he noticed the small wince of pain as she settled inside the car.

"We'll stop by and pick up some of your things," he explained. "Then we're going to my cabin."

"What?" The look of surprise on Olivia's face would have been funny had the obvious refusal in her eyes not cut him to the bone. Was he so repulsive that she couldn't imagine spending the night in his cabin? Or was it her disdain for his work?

Or the fact that you let her father get killed?

"Don't be unreasonable, Olivia. Not only was your apartment trashed, but someone tried to gun you down. Do you really think it's the safest place to recuperate?"

Her face grew more strained, her voice resigned. "I...guess not. But why don't you take me to a hotel?"

"Because you're officially in protective custody."

"You mean you want to watch over me so I don't get in your way?"

"You're obviously feeling more like yourself today," he growled. "Testy. Argumentative. Impossible."

She glowered at him as she pushed her disheveled blond hair from her face. His sex hardened, his hands itching to assume the task for her, to smooth the silky strands into place himself.

Instead, he clenched the steering wheel and refused to look at her the rest of the way to her apartment. Where was the Iceman? He needed him back, now more than ever.

"Oh, my God." Olivia staggered at the sight of the vandalism the intruder had wrought as Craig escorted her into her apartment. Her drawers were open and had been pawed through, her books and file cabinet tossed as if someone had been searching for something, her computer smashed.

"I...have to get another computer."

"I'll have one sent over."

She glanced at him, her surprise obvious. "You will?"

"Look, Olivia, I told you we were going to work together. I may not like your job, or any of the media for that matter, but I'm a man of my word."

"You hate the media. It's because of your father, isn't it?" Olivia leaned against the sofa, battling another dizzy spell. "Why? Because of all the publicity about your sister's death?"

He froze, anger knotting every muscle in his body. "What do you know about my sister's death?"

She inhaled sharply. "Just that it came at a bad time for your father's campaign. Or maybe it made it easier for him to run for office. He needed the escape."

"Just like your father needed work to escape the pain of losing your mother?" he asked.

She swallowed hard, then nodded. "I imagine the senator's opponent took advantage of your family's grief, but then again, your father won some sympathy votes to even it out. But I don't think the real story about your sister was ever printed. Your father probably paid someone to keep it quiet, didn't he?"

God, she was honest. He didn't know whether to admire her or be offended that she'd checked on him. "The media were vultures," he said between gritted teeth, remembering a female one in particular. He'd let down his guard during pillow talk, voiced his anger and grief, blamed his father for neglecting his sister...and she'd printed every word.

"My sister died in a car accident," he said in a deep voice. "End of story."

The questions in her eyes rankled him, as did her long unwavering look of distrust, although he didn't know why. He shouldn't care if she trusted him or liked him.

Hadn't he vowed not to fall into the same trap with her as he had with the other woman...what was her name? He couldn't even remember anymore.

"I'll get a service to clean the apartment," he said, obviously trying to change the subject.

"No, I can do it here—"

"I promised the doctor you'd rest, and I intend to see to it that you do." His tone brooked no argument.

She stared at him for another long moment, as if she were trying to read between the lines, but he refused to give her the opportunity.

"All right," she finally agreed. "But only because I want to reserve my energy for the investigation."

That grit of hers again. He almost smiled but choked it back. "I'll wait here while you pack."

She nodded and hurried to her bedroom, picking her way over the magazines and papers strewn on the floor. He followed but remained at the door, noting the hint of her femininity in the white eyelet comforter on her iron bed. Hmm, another interesting layer to the gutsy woman. One he'd like to explore.

One he definitely wouldn't.

Still, he hadn't envisioned her room as traditional or frilly. A Victorian lamp sat on a nightstand with a ruffled red-and-yellow striped skirt. Balloon shades in the same fabric hung above the windows. A lacy white robe lay on top of the bed, and her lingerie drawer was spilling over with flimsy silk and lace bikini panties, thongs and a teddy in black that made perspiration break out on his forehead and neck.

He pivoted away, forcing the image of Olivia in that black teddy from his mind, although the traitorous thought kept flashing back, tormenting him with *what-ifs*.

What if they weren't working on a case? What if she wasn't in danger? What if they weren't on opposite sides? What if she wasn't a reporter?

Then he might take her to bed. Peel away the layers of her multifaceted personality and that tough facade and touch the silky softness beneath.

But if they weren't on a case, they never would have met....

"I'm ready."

He schooled his reaction to the sound of her whispery voice, snapping his air of brusque control back in place as they walked back to the police car.

Ten minutes later, they arrived at his cabin, and he helped her out, then thanked the officer. The natural overhang of live oaks shaded the cabin, the sound of the ocean waves crashing against the rocks almost symphonic.

"It's nice," Olivia said, pausing to inhale the fresh, salty air. "Not what I expected."

His jaw snapped tight. "What did you think, that I'd live in a hovel?"

She laughed, then pressed a hand against her side as if the movement hurt. "No. More like a steel-gray contemporary condo."

Perfect for the Iceman, the image he normally evoked, he thought. But he didn't pursue the topic; he simply pushed inside, let her enter, then grabbed her suitcase.

He gestured toward the bedroom. "You can stay in my room. I'll take the sofa."

She caught his arm. "Craig, I can't do that."

"For God's sake, Olivia, do you have to argue with everything?"

He hadn't meant to speak so harshly, but the sudden set to her jaw indicated his tone had forced renewed distance between them. Distance he needed now that she was in his home.

Because letting her sleep in his bed would be difficult.

Letting her sleep there alone—paramount to torture.

OLIVIA RETREATED TO the small bedroom, ignoring the stab of hurt she'd felt at Craig's tone. Their situation was impossible. Could she really stay here and work? She didn't want Craig looking over her shoulder.

She wanted him holding her hand again. Soothing her. Stroking her. Kissing her.

Which was ridiculous.

Olivia Thornbird didn't need anyone.

Suddenly exhausted and weak, she stretched out on the denim-covered oak bed. The room appeared masculine, suited him more than the empty sterile steel-gray place she'd imagined, made her think of what he would look like sprawled on the bed beside her. Naked and muscular with dark hair sprinkled across his legs and chest—

"Olivia?"

Startled, she looked up guiltily, hoping her feelings weren't written all over her face. He stood in the shadows, his look brooding, but his broad shoulders were so wide she ached to rush into them.

Then he moved toward her, approached the bed and stared down at her. Seconds lapsed into a tension-fraught minute as his eyes flared with something that looked like desire. "If you need anything, just let me know."

His husky offer triggered dark memories. The horrors of the night returned. The nightmares. The morgue. But that voice also elicited tremors of sexual awareness, thoughts of heated touches and pleasures known only between a man and woman in the heat of a lonely night.

Unable to resist, she reached up, took his hand and pulled him down beside her. One second, she just wanted to thank him, the next she was in his arms wanting so much more.

He cradled her face so gently that tears nearly spilled from her eyes. After a low groan of protest, his lips met hers, softly, gently teasing, exploring, and she sighed and threaded her fingers through his hair. He groaned again, this time deep and throaty, welcoming, then deepened the kiss, his tongue meeting hers to dance and stir the need within her. Sensations raced through her, cutting off rational sense as she parted her lips and welcomed him inside. He traced a finger over her jaw, teasing her with fire as he stoked the flames already flaring up between them. She pulled him closer, met his tongue thrust for thrust, ached to have him closer, his bare skin next to hers. His hand touched her bandage, and he froze. She winced, and he pulled away slightly.

"God, what are we doing?" he mumbled.

The self-loathing in his voice twisted her insides.

"It's all right," she whispered.

"No," he snapped. "You're injured. We have to maintain a professional relationship."

A relationship that was tentative and shaky at best. But the sex between them wouldn't be tentative. It would be volatile, explosive....

He set her away from him. "That kiss was a mistake, Olivia. It can't happen again."

She swallowed hard. Rarely did she ever ask for anything, especially comfort. She should have known Craig Horn was the last man on earth who'd give it.

He stood abruptly as if he couldn't get away from her fast enough. "I brought you here to keep you safe, not to have sex with you. I'll let you rest now."

She nodded slowly, although she wanted to tell him not to leave her again. But she'd already begged him once. Once more than she'd ever begged in her life.

His cold referral to the sexual heat between them doused the flame of desire lingering within her. Angry at him for turning the moment into some kind of sordid, tawdry, worthless physical act, she shot back, "Believe me, Agent Horn, I came here to work on this case, not seduce you."

"Fine," he snapped in a steel-edged voice.

"Yes, fine."

He spun around and left, closing the door behind him, shutting the door on any kind of emotion.

She closed her eyes, wondering if she'd imagined the heat between them. She was a fool for throwing herself at him.

He was just like her parents. Obsessed with work. Unable to give emotionally.

And she had to remember it.

She'd vowed to never let anyone get close enough to hurt her again. And Craig Horn, the federal agent who'd caused her father's death by involving him in this investigation, the Iceman, was the last man on earth she would break that vow for.

But even as she fell asleep in his bed, the smell of him on the pillow and the subtle reminder of his sexuality teased her senses, the kiss lingered in her memory and her body ached for more.

No one knew where Olivia was. She was safe in his house. Asleep.

And he was better off leaving her for a while before he gave in to temptation and kissed her again or did more.

Reminding himself she would be all right at his cabin, that no one knew her location, Craig met Detective Black at the precinct to interrogate Harlam Jones, a man who'd recently been paroled after spending five years in jail for starting an anthrax scare by sending fake chemicals to various people's homes as a practical joke.

"I told the cops, it was just a freaking joke," Harlam declared.

"And no one thought it was funny." Craig zeroed in on the tattoos marking his arms. "Are those your initiation to an inside prison gang?"

Harlam snorted. "I've had these since I was fifteen. The only thing I got in the pen was scars." He lifted the edge of his shirt to reveal a smattering of knife wounds and jagged puckered flesh. "Since I got out, I'm trying to stay clean."

"Are you sure you don't have a grudge against the Savannah Police Department for locking you up?" Craig asked.

"Yeah, maybe you're sending around the real thing this time," Detective Black said.

Harlam popped up in his chair, pulling at his hair. "You mean someone's sending out anthrax and you think it's me?" The vile words he uttered would have blistered paint. "That ain't so, I tell you, I ain't done nothing wrong."

"That's what you said before," Detective Black said.

"But this time it's the truth. Ask my old lady. She's been keeping me under lock and key, makes me hand off that pitiful paycheck to her. I don't have the money to buy a pack of freaking cigarettes without asking her, much less buy some kind of drug."

"Do you know anyone who might be selling off the street?" Detective Black asked.

"You mean pot? Crack? Heroine?"

Craig gave him a steady gaze. "We're not after narcotics."

Harlam clawed at his arms as if he were frantic to escape. "Then you mean anthrax."

Craig leered in his face. "How about a germ similar to anthrax?"

"You're talking some scary stuff," Harlam yelled, his eye twitching. "I don't know nothing about it, I swear."

Craig glanced at Black, frustrated. They were getting nowhere. And if Harlam's nerves were any indication of his innocence, this was a waste of time.

Time they couldn't afford to waste, although they had to exhaust every possibility.

"Bring his wife in," he told Detective Black. "Let's see what she has to say."

Harlam buried his head in his arms and groaned, as if he'd just received a death sentence.

But thirty minutes later, after Harlam's wife corroborated his statement, Craig and Black agreed they had to release the man.

"I'll put a tail on him anyway," Black said.

Craig agreed, then decided to cut Harlam a deal. "Listen, go out there on the street and see if you hear word of anyone dealing something besides drugs, something like anthrax."

Harlam swallowed hard, his eyes bulging. "And what you gonna do for me?"

"Maybe we'll forget that I smelled booze on your breath when you came in, that you like to knock one back before you go home from work."

Harlam nodded. Drinking alcohol violated his parole. He obviously didn't want to go back into the pen.

TWO HOURS LATER, when Olivia awakened, a laptop had been placed on the oak desk. Craig had fulfilled his promise.

Was he really as trustworthy as he appeared?

She washed her face in the small bathroom, the scent of his aftershave wafting toward her, the sight of his personal toiletries reminding her of the intimacy of their arrangement. An intimacy she couldn't take to another level.

Not when there was so much at stake. She'd wanted to find the answers to her mother's death all her life. And now her father's. She had to know the truth.

She booted up the computer and spent a half hour retrieving her work files. Finally, when she'd skimmed the paper's recent articles, one of her attempted murder on page three, again written by her nemesis and co-worker Jerry, she logged on to the Internet and punched in the name Martin Shubert.

Knowing he was a doctor helped to narrow her search. Still, there were three different listings for doctors with the same name. She cross-checked them with scientists who'd worked on assignments in Egypt the same time as her mother but found nothing. Next, she tried CIRP, but Shubert hadn't worked there, wasn't affiliated with them or someone had deleted any references to him from the files.

Which was possible since they kept so much of their work secret.

She tapped her nails on her leg. How would she ever find the truth with the security measures in place on Nighthawk Island?

"HORN, IT'S DEVLIN."

"Yeah, what have you found?"

"It appears the scientists here in Europe have a similar strain of the virus that affected the Savannah victims. It has mutated slightly, but could have originated from the same source."

"Do we know how the patients were infected?"

"Not yet. We've cordoned off the residences and work areas of each of the victims and are testing the air, walls, anything in the space which might hold bacteria."

"I thought we already determined that it wasn't airborne."

Devlin cleared his throat. "We did, but it's possible that the germ might have settled inside the framework, so we're double-checking."

In other words, they were grasping. Craig explained about the attack on Olivia at the hospital.

"Jeez. She must have gotten too close to something," Devlin said. "Find out what she knows."

Craig swallowed, then glanced at the bedroom door. The earlier kiss taunted him; the fact that Olivia was asleep in his bed was driving him crazy. But what if she was holding back information? "I will."

"I spoke with a contact here," Devlin said. "He suggested Thornbird might have been more involved with the virus than we thought."

"You mean he found something?"

A long pause, then Devlin sighed. "We have to consider the possibility that he might have been the one who actually created the germ in the first place. When you asked for help, he jumped at the chance."

"Yes." Craig hesitated, contemplated the possibility. "So he could throw us off?"

"Exactly."

"Then Thornbird might be responsible for all these people's deaths."

"Right," Devlin said. "And his own."

"Because he knew we might be on to him."

"Exactly." Devlin whistled. "See if Olivia had any idea what her father was up to. Maybe if she knows something, we can pressure her to be a government witness."

Horn clenched the phone with sweaty hands as Olivia stepped from the shadows. Her face was haunted with exhaustion, the memory of his lips on hers stirring unwanted desires.

"All right." Anger knotted his stomach as distrust rose from the bowels of that desire, and another what-if popped into his mind.

What if she had known her father had created the virus, and she'd warmed up to him to keep him from finding out the truth? Had she sneaked into her father's office so she could cover for him…destroy his files?

Chapter Nine

Craig's head was still reeling when he hung up from talking to Devlin. He'd done it again. Started to trust a woman. And all because of a pair of sexy blue eyes and a kiss that had twisted him inside out.

A snort of derision left him. Good thing Devlin had yanked the chain on that idiocy.

But what if Olivia didn't know that her father might have been involved in creating the virus? What if she was innocent? Would he be able to tell her the truth and hurt her like that?

Don't let those bewitching eyes fool you. She's not so innocent. She's an investigative reporter.

He angled his head, searched for hidden secrets in her eyes, but haunted shadows lingered from her earlier ordeal.

The facts—he had to go on what he knew so far. Someone definitely wanted her dead. Either they believed she was a threat, that she was on to the truth, or that she already knew something. They were probably afraid she'd write the story and lead the cops back to the source.

Even if her father had created the virus, he hadn't orchestrated this plan alone. But he'd obviously been crazy to go along with it.

Had he invented the virus for germ warfare, then sold it to the wrong people? And if he had, had he known? Or had someone stolen it from him?

The possibilities were endless. Even if Thornbird hadn't intentionally given the virus to the person or persons responsible for the outbreak, he might have figured out what had happened. And the guilt of knowing he'd played a part in murdering innocent citizens might have driven Thornbird to suicide.

Craig needed to dig deeper into Thornbird's relationship with his daughter.

"Craig, what's going on?" Olivia asked.

"I just spoke with Devlin. They're retesting the facilities where the victims lived and worked to see if the virus might have settled in the vents or become embedded in the materials or structural foundation. It's just a precaution."

"Then they'll check my father's house?"

"Yes." He shifted. "Olivia, were there any stories you worked on recently that might have pissed off someone enough to want to harm you?"

She leaned against the doorway, her posture evident of the strain of her surgery. "Not really. I was investigating a story about the acrylic nail business. The possibility that the chemicals imported in vats from Asia are potentially hazardous to one's health."

He quirked a brow. "Do you have proof?"

"Not yet. But there's some evidence that the chemicals are definitely harmful to pregnant women when it's absorbed through the skin. And if ingested, it might prove lethal or cause birth defects."

"How or why would someone ingest nail chemicals?"

"Some women chew on their nails, even the acrylic ones. But we're still talking minimal ingestion then."

He frowned. "Any of the owners in particular come to mind?"

"No, but I've only scratched the surface. I don't think anyone's going to kill me over the story."

"What else?"

"I've made contact with an inside source investigating potential gang problems in the school system. So far, though, I haven't written anything up."

His admiration rose a notch.

"That's the only two big stories I have at the moment. The rest have been coverage of local crimes."

"Can you give me the name of the undercover cop?"

She shook her head, her long hair falling across one cheek. "I won't reveal my source to anyone, Craig. It might endanger him."

He wasn't surprised. "But you're sure you can trust this cop?"

"Absolutely. He's putting his life on the line to infiltrate the gang. He's close, but it'll take time for him to get to the leader."

"Have you received any threats?"

Another hesitation, and he knew the truth.

His hand hit the table. "When?"

She chewed her bottom lip, massaging her elbow where it was braced in the sling across her left shoulder. "Just one. A phone call yesterday morning."

He grunted. "Why didn't you mention it?"

"I thought it might be a crank call."

He paced in front of the window, heard the sound of the ocean crashing against the rocky shore and knew the turbulent tides mirrored the emotions raging inside him. "Damn it, you can't take chances like that, Olivia. Even if you don't think it's serious, I want to know if you receive any more threats. Understood?"

"Yes," she said wearily.

Shadows from the window darkened the room, the dwindling sunlight dappling golden hues with the murky gray. With dusk setting and the long night looming ahead, he had to rein in his emotions. Too much could happen between them when night fell, too many temptations…

"So we're back to the virus and suicide cases," Craig said. "Have you questioned anyone besides Hall?"

"Hal Oberman, the head of the DPS."

Craig froze, mentally replaying his conversation with Oberman. Oberman wanted Craig to take care of Olivia, had told him to do whatever he needed to do to keep her quiet.

"And I tried contacting your father," Olivia said, "but of course he refused my calls."

"He's a busy man," Craig said, although he knew the excuse sounded weak.

"He supports germ warfare," Olivia countered.

Craig's chest tightened, another possibility nagging at him, although he didn't want to even contemplate that his father might be involved. But Olivia was right. His dad believed the government should protect themselves by actively pursuing germ warfare research. If the scientists on Nighthawk Island had created this virus, did his father know about it?

The fine hairs along the back of his neck stood on end.

And if he did, and the germ had accidentally fallen into the wrong hands causing these deaths, what lengths would he and the government go to in order to cover up their involvement?

OLIVIA STUDIED THE TIGHT SET to Craig's jaw and wondered why he'd tensed. Did his father know something about the germ virus research that he didn't want revealed?

Her cell phone jangled, and she reached for her purse, the ache in her arm and shoulder reminding her it was time for a pain pill. But she hated to take medication. She wanted to be alert.

She snapped open the phone. "Hello. Olivia Thornbird."

"Olivia, thank God. It's Jerry."

"Jerry?" What did he want? To take pictures of her half-incapacitated for another story?

Craig moved closer so she covered the mouthpiece and whispered, "It's my co-worker from the paper."

He nodded and stepped into the kitchen nook to give her privacy.

She turned back to the phone, grateful to be away from Craig's probing eyes. "What's up, Jerry?"

"We've been worried sick about you at the paper. Where are you? I've called and Carter drove by your house."

Olivia bit her lip. Carter was just antsy for a story. "The federal agent in charge of the Savannah Suicides case thought it would be best if I didn't go home. I'm staying at…a cabin."

"Oh, that makes sense." Jerry hesitated. "Listen, I need to see you. Can I stop by?"

Olivia gave him the address, then disconnected, surprised at the concern in Jerry's voice. Although once or twice he'd suggested they have drinks, she hadn't considered that he was interested in her. She'd assumed he'd just wanted to outscoop her on a story.

The smell of food cooking wafted toward her, and she walked toward the kitchen. Craig was stir-frying vegetables in a pan. Mushroom, onions, green peppers, broccoli—her stomach growled. The morning's pasty hospital oatmeal had been inedible. "You cook?"

He scowled. "When I'm not eating raw meat."

She rubbed her arm, almost laughing at his deadpan answer. But the heat from the kitchen was as steamy as the heat rising between them. Craig Horn, all rumpled in the kitchen, was an unnerving sight. "I'm sorry. I...just didn't see you as domestic."

His eyes skated over her. Dark. Seductive. "How do you see me, Olivia?"

A loaded question. Sexy. Tough. Mysterious. Brooding. Naked.

"Olivia?"

"As a federal agent, of course," she said instead. "Cold. Calculating. Mysterious. Suspicious of everyone and everything."

"With good reason." He snorted, although a second later a small smile tugged at the corner of his mouth, morphing him from the enigmatic Iceman she'd believed him to be into something much more dangerous. Much sexier.

The air grew even hotter. When he wasn't chasing

criminals, this man was probably seducing women with his dark air and that killer smile. He'd shed his suit jacket and holster, even loosened the tie at his neck. Forgetting for a moment the danger that faced them, the reason she was here, her mind took a dangerous journey, and she mentally undressed him the rest of the way. Imagined his broad chest dusted in dark hair. His narrow waist tapering to firm hips. The dark thatch of hair surrounding his sex…

He cleared his throat. "What's wrong?"

She shook her head, embarrassed at her train of thought. "Nothing. Can I help?"

His eyes met hers again, the memory of that kiss heating her bloodstream, sizzling hotter than the vegetables in the pan. "Grab some plates and glasses. There's a bottle of wine in the fridge. It's already uncorked."

Wine might dull the ache, better than a pain pill. She busied herself getting the table settings, then found two wineglasses and poured them both a drink. The chardonnay tasted perfect, not too sweet, not too tart. But as the clear liquid rolled off her tongue and slid down her throat, she thought of kisses. Tasting his mouth.

Don't go there, Olivia. You have too much work to do to think about sex.

You're only here because someone tried to kill you. And because your father is dead.

The sobering thought brought reality crashing back just as he opened the oven door and removed two salmon steaks. "I hope you eat seafood."

"It smells delicious."

The muggy air engulfed them as he served the plates, and they sat down at the table. His masculine body suddenly took up too much space. They bumped elbows as they both reached for the salt, the tension so thick she could hear his every breath.

The wine might have been a mistake, too—she was beginning to feel mellow, all languid and warm inside. She wondered if she'd have this same insane attraction to him if danger hadn't brought them together. If she'd be just as drawn to him…

The doorbell cut into the quiet, thankfully preventing her from making a fool out of herself by acting on the attraction brewing between them. He frowned and reached for his gun, tucking it into the waistband of his slacks.

"That's probably Jerry, my co-worker at the paper. He said he was going to stop by."

He gripped her wrist. "Why the hell did you tell him where you were?"

She stiffened. "For goodness sake, Craig. He works with me."

"You're here because you're under protective custody, Olivia. That means you tell no one your location."

"But—"

"Protective custody," he barked. "We can't trust anyone right now."

She swallowed, shoving aside the wine, his tone a firm reminder that he was right. She couldn't trust anyone. If it served his purpose, Craig would hide things from her in the end.

And she couldn't trust herself, either, especially when it came to wanting him.

CRAIG GAVE JERRY RENARD a skeptical once-over as he entered, automatically disliking the scrawny man. Not only was he a reporter with a jaded slant to his articles, especially any piece involving the government, but he'd personally written derogatory articles about Craig's father. And his latest piece about the Savannah Suicides had painted a picture of the locals and feds as being incompetent.

He also wanted Olivia.

The smarmy smile on his face was obviously meant to be charming. The sleaze had even brought a bouquet of flowers, balloons and a box of chocolates.

"I come bearing gifts," Jerry said as he greeted Olivia with a kiss to her cheek.

"I can't believe you did this." Olivia's surprise seemed sincere, although the smile that lit her eyes proved she was flattered. Score one point for Jerry.

Jerry held out the gifts. "Everyone at the paper was worried about you."

"Thank you." Olivia wrapped the string of balloons around the edge of the desk chair, placed the flowers in a glass of water, and ripped open the chocolates. "You shouldn't have done this. You know I'm trying to give them up."

Renard laughed, a deep throaty chuckle that suggested intimate secrets, and Craig ground his molars. Fisting his hands by his side, he cleared his throat, jerking attention to him.

"I'm addicted to chocolate," she explained. "Breakfast, lunch and dinner."

Craig moved closer to her, aware he was acting territorial. He told himself it was his job. He was simply protecting Olivia.

"Carter says to take all the time you need," Renard said. "We have things under control at the paper."

"Tell Carter I'm working, too." She wiped a drop of the dark truffle from her mouth, then laughed. The sound took Craig off guard—she certainly hadn't laughed with *him.* Although it was a good thing. The sound heated his bloodstream to a fever pitch.

"Do you have a story yet?" Renard asked.

"No," Craig answered for her.

"Do you know who tried to gun you down?" Renard asked.

"Not yet," Olivia said. "But I will. And soon."

Craig's phone trilled, and he frowned, hesitant to leave Olivia alone with her co-worker. But Detective Black's number appeared, so he stepped into the kitchen to answer it.

"Agent Horn, we've got another one," Detective Black said. "Twenty-six-year-old male. Shot himself with a .38."

Damn. "Where?"

"Skidaway Island." Black recited the address.

"I'll be right there."

OLIVIA COULD BARELY force herself to pay attention to Jerry for wondering who had phoned Craig.

"I'll be glad to pick up the slack for you, Olivia—"

"Excuse me, Renard, you have to go."

Olivia swung around as Craig strode into the room. His gray eyes cut a scathing path toward her. Predatory. Possessive. Demanding. Like some kind of male animal drawing a battle line in the sand.

She started to protest. "But—"

"I'm sorry," Craig said, cutting off her protest. "Olivia, you need to rest."

She glared at him. "I'm perfectly capable of deciding when I need to rest and when I don't."

He gripped her arm. "I promised the doctor I'd watch you, and I intend to follow through." He gestured toward the door. "You can let yourself out, Renny."

"It's Renard," the man said.

Craig shrugged, but Olivia pulled away from Craig, offered Jerry an apologetic look and walked him to the door. "Thanks for dropping by."

He brushed her cheek with the pad of his thumb. "I meant what I said, Olivia. If you need anything, call."

She gripped the handle, uncertain whether she trusted his motives. And she certainly didn't trust or understand Craig Horn.

Furious with his Machiavellian conduct, she turned, ready to blast him, but he cut her off.

"There's been another suicide, Olivia," he said in a clipped tone. "We have to go."

She exhaled slowly. So he hadn't been making a statement about her at all. Disappointment slammed into her, although she didn't understand why. She didn't want Craig acting possessive over her, making demands. "I see. So I'm going with you?"

"I sure as hell can't leave you here. You'd probably put an announcement in the paper and lead the killer to the door."

Irritation crawled through her. "I'm not an idiot, Craig."

He gestured toward the chocolates. "No, neither am I. And I don't trust your co-worker."

Olivia raised a brow, but he didn't elaborate.

"And remember the deal. You can go with me, but you can't print anything until I give you the go-ahead."

She nodded and followed him outside, pulling at her clothes as the stifling heat matted them to her body. She wanted to ask Craig why he'd taken such an instant disliking to Jerry, then wrote off his behavior as the Iceman. He didn't need friends.

Didn't want her as one or as a lover.

Shutting out the thought, she rode with him in silence, her mind ticking over the details of the case, searching for anything that might help them. Twenty minutes later, they surveyed the exterior of the crime scene, a small bungalow on the corner of Skidaway Island. Heat melded her hair to her forehead, the wind bringing the pungent odor of salt and fish. Craig was aloof, businesslike, back to his brooding self. But at least he hadn't forced her to remain in the car, although, as he donned protective clothing before entering the house, he ordered her to stay close by the local detectives and refused to allow her entrance.

Olivia balked, but then spotted a woman in jeans and a T-shirt crying on the sidewalk. She headed toward her to find out what she knew.

OLIVIA THORNBIRD MUST HAVE nine lives.

He blended into the backdrop of trees bordering the Rucker property, a chuckle building in his chest as he watched the slew of health-care workers, FBI and cops swarming the small bungalow, scurrying around to figure out the reason for this rash of suicides.

The fact that the CDC was on the case proved they'd

caught on to one thing though—the deaths weren't exactly suicides.

Then again, they couldn't prove anything yet. And even when they did, his hands were clean. The disease had actually driven the victims to take their own lives.

The perfect murder.

Olivia Thornbird would be next.

Had she received the little present he'd sent her?

One truffle would be enough to infect her. Several, and her health would rapidly deteriorate.

Ironic—Special Agent Craig Horn had taken her into protective custody to keep her safe, yet she'd probably die right in his house with him watching.

Feeling helpless. Guilty. Responsible.

But unable to do anything to prevent it.

Chapter Ten

As Olivia approached the woman, Detective Clayton Fox stepped toward her. "Miss Thornbird, we don't want the press here—"

"I'm here with Agent Horn." She gestured toward Craig. "Ask him. We made a deal. I get the story, but I won't print anything specific until he clears it."

Detective Fox radioed his partner, Detective Black, who thankfully confirmed her story. Still, he stood nearby, his eyes glued to her like a hawk as she introduced herself to the woman.

"Miss, my name is Olivia Thornbird."

"I'm Tanya Miller. Are you a cop?"

"No, ma'am, I work for the newspaper." Olivia joined her on the curb, lowering her voice to a sympathetic pitch. "I'm sorry for your loss. How did you know Mr. Rucker?"

Tears streamed down her chubby cheeks like twin rivers. "He was my…fiancé." Tanya shoved red hair from her face and took a shaky breath, then knotted her hands in her lap. "I don't understand why Alvin would kill himself. We were going to be married in three weeks."

Olivia's heart squeezed at the anguish in her voice. Only two days ago, she'd sat in this woman's place. She reached out and rubbed her back. "I'm so sorry, Tanya. I understand what you're going through. I...lost my father to suicide like this, too."

Tanya jerked her eyes toward Olivia. "He's the man I read about in the paper?"

"Yes." Olivia still couldn't believe he was gone. And fatigue was setting in although she fought it. "Did you notice anything odd about your fiancé's behavior lately?" she asked quietly. "Was he moody? Depressed?"

Tanya wiped her tears with the back of her hand, and Olivia retrieved a tissue from her purse and stuffed it in her hand.

Tanya's chin wobbled. "I thought maybe it was the wedding, that he'd gotten cold feet. When I tried to talk to him about it, he snapped my head off."

"Had he been physically sick?"

"Not that I know of." She dried her eyes. "Well, although now that you mention it, he did complain of headaches. And he had a strange rash on his arms and chest."

The same symptoms as her father and the other victims.

Tanya sniffed. "And last night when I called, he was acting odd. He kept ranting about a government conspiracy, that people were after him."

"What did your boyfriend do for a living?"

"He was a construction worker, so what he said didn't make sense." She wadded the tissue in her hands. "He was going to build our first...house."

Olivia patted her again. All the more reason to find out who was behind his death and put a stop to it.

Grateful her left shoulder had been shot instead of her right, Olivia removed a pen and pad and jotted notes, uncertain if anything would help at this point. But they couldn't discount any clue, no matter how trivial it appeared to be at the time.

Tanya dried her eyes again, then seemed to become more aware of her surroundings. Her face scrunched with worry. "Why are all those people wearing protective clothing?"

Detective Fox had been watching, listening to her conversation. Olivia knew he'd already questioned the woman and had probably tried to abate her concerns, but Tanya obviously realized something was being kept from her.

"It's just a precautionary measure," Olivia said, although the sight of the health-care workers definitely would incite panic if a photo of them appeared in the paper. Her reporter instincts kicked in. She was tempted to call for a cameraman, wanted to warn the public that they might be dealing with a deadly virus, that the cops had no idea how people were being infected.

But Craig Horn exited the bungalow, his unnerving gaze sliding toward her, and a shiver rippled through her. The memory of their kiss returned. The deal they'd cut. The cold, unforgiving way he acted most of the time. The scent of his body on his pillow.

The feel of his lips on hers.

A web of worries, questions and emotions tangled inside her, followed by exhaustion.

Could she keep the promise she'd made to him and remain quiet?

WHEN CRAIG EXITED THE HOUSE, he removed the protective clothing and mask in the area designated for the health-care workers, then scanned the perimeter, silently grateful they'd been able to keep the press away from this crime scene.

His gaze zeroed in on Olivia. She was standing next to the dead man's fiancé. Asking questions. Doing her job.

He hated her work, but he admired her drive.

And God help him. She looked tired and needed rest but he wanted the woman. Bad.

Maybe more than he ever had another female.

Would she keep her vow not to publish the story until they had time to find the answers, or had she lied?

He spotted the contact from the CDC and made his way toward the man. "Dr. Carrington?"

"Yes?"

"Special Agent Horn. FBI. We spoke on the phone."

"Yes, nice to meet you."

"What do you think we're dealing with here?" Craig asked.

Carrington scrubbed a hand over his cap, thick curly gray hair protruding from the edges. "I wish to God I knew." His accent was Midwestern. "Hopefully my team will have answers about the virus soon."

Craig nodded. "I'm going to CIRP tomorrow to question Thornbird's co-workers."

"If you get a copy of his research, fax it over. Any findings he had, even strains he'd eliminated, would expedite our process." Carrington hesitated. "I spoke with Oberman from the DPS. The last of the soil and water samples came back clean."

Craig agreed to stay in touch, said goodbye and

headed toward Olivia. It was past midnight, the fatigue lines on her face reminding him that she was recovering from a gunshot wound and a near fatal drug-induced heart attack, not to mention she was still grieving over her father.

There was nothing more he could do here tonight. The locals were canvassing the area, questioning neighbors. Others patrolled the beach behind the bungalow, but so far they'd discovered no one suspicious. He'd even phoned the psychologist, Dr. Janine Woodward, to see if Rucker had been a patient, but he hadn't, so that eliminated the only connection they'd found so far.

How had four different people from four different walks of life, four parts of the city with no jobs or friends in common, contracted this virus?

"Remember the mail-bomb scare a while back?" he said to Detective Black. "Maybe we're dealing with something like that now."

"I'll have officers collect any mail the victim received and we'll check it," the detective assured him.

Craig nodded, explained that he'd visit CIRP the next day, then went to take Olivia home before she passed out.

Or before she said too much and asked more questions. Questions he didn't know how to answer.

OLIVIA STRUGGLED TO STAY awake on the ride back to Craig's, but the few sips of wine she'd consumed at dinnertime combined with the aftereffects of her surgery and exhaustion claimed her.

"Olivia?"

She roused and reached for the door handle, but felt herself being lifted and carried toward the cabin.

"Craig, I can walk."

"Hush. I'm tired and I don't want to wait on you to drag yourself out of the car."

She grumbled but thought she detected a note of teasing in his voice and wondered if she was delusional. A few minutes later, she stirred as he placed her on the bed. Cool air brushed her shoulders as he lifted her arm from the sling and started to remove her shirt.

"No." She clutched the sling, suddenly self-conscious. A feeling she didn't like.

"I'm just trying to help, Olivia."

She placed her fingers over his. "I can undress myself."

He hesitated, his hands stilling on her shoulders, his breath brushing her cheek. The air felt sultry, the scent of his masculinity teasing her nerve endings. She imagined him peeling away her clothes, tracing his finger over her bare skin, and shivered. But she had an ugly wound now...

"Are you sure?" he asked in a gruff voice.

No, she wasn't sure of anything. Except that she wanted him to kiss her again. To touch her and soothe away the pain of the last few days.

"Yes, I'm sure. But thanks, Craig. You've been...kind."

He growled a protest. "You're the stubbornest woman I know."

She smiled into the dark and waited until he left the room to collapse onto the bed. As much as she wanted to undress, she was too tired to struggle through the motions. Besides, her shoulder was throbbing like hell.

But she'd never admit it to Craig.

Because if she did, she might reveal her true self and admit that she wanted him to lie down beside her, to

make her forget that a serial murderer or terrorist was killing unsuspecting people. That he'd killed her only remaining family member. That he was after her.

And that being alone frightened her more than death itself.

FOUR PEOPLE had died now.

Four people too many.

Craig hardened himself against the reminder, the guilt weighing him down. If he'd done his job, it would have stopped at one. But he was missing something.

Something right under his nose.

Frustrated and unable to sleep for thinking about Olivia in his bed, from imagining her naked and doing things to his body that would make him forget his job, at least for one night, he booted up his computer and forced himself to focus on the case. The occasional breeze fluttering through the window from the bedroom brought her scent to him, enticing him to forget his research and join her in bed. He imagined the subtle curves that lay beneath her clothes, the slope of her back and spine, the tender skin where he would kiss her and make her squirm.

Irritated, he stood, grabbed a beer and forced the images from his mind as he typed in her father's name. Thornbird had a degree from Harvard, had completed postdoctoral work at Emory Medical Center, had worked for various research companies before joining CIRP.

Several references to a doctor named Fulton popped up, the same man who was working the case now, studying Thornbird's files. Fulton had been given a medical discharge from the service after injuries sustained in a recon military mission years ago and had worked on government projects since. Hmm, could he be working on germ warfare research?

He turned back to the file. Thornbird had no criminal record, not even a parking ticket. According to recent articles, he had received an award for work he'd conducted on infectious diseases, had worked on researching Agent Orange as well as identifying two strains of viruses brought in from other countries that had characteristics similar to SARS.

So far, nothing shady to indicate the man would have sold a germ virus to a foreign country.

Except for his wife's death.

He read further and learned that Ruth Thornbird had researched germ warfare long before it became a hot topic. On her last mission, she'd supposedly traveled to Egypt to eradicate polio and help educate other countries on proper vaccinations. One journalist speculated that the trip was a front, that Ruth had discovered a rare and unusual virus that the government had been working on at the time, a project called Y-3X which the government had refused to discuss. The paper had been sued for the story; the reporter had been fired and then he had disappeared.

Craig leaned back, rubbing his temple with his thumb, contemplating the possibilities. What if the same thing had happened to Thornbird? Or what if Thornbird had discovered his wife's involvement in germ warfare research and had been killed to keep him quiet? But if so, why wait fifteen years?

Unless he'd been party to the unethical germ warfare experiments at the time and now a similar germ had surfaced—maybe he had created both strains.

And maybe Thornbird had orchestrated the murder of his own wife.

The possibility intrigued Craig, and might offer a lot of answers. Answers that would hurt Olivia.

He had to know if Olivia was involved. What exactly she knew.

Her visit from Renard flashed back, and he entered the reporter's name, then ran a background check, his suspicions mounting. Renard had been to Iraq and Afghanistan, had witnessed the devastation of suicide bombings, had covered the stories of lost lives. How had he felt about returning stateside and being handed local stories? Or had he come to Savannah so he could specifically research CIRP?

Maybe he knew more than he was letting on.

Or…he could have traveled overseas and been working with a terrorist group there. If so, he might have brought the virus back with him.

He scratched his head, wondering if his imagination was going wild or if his theories held credence. If so, how much did Olivia know? And how much could he chance telling her without blowing the case?

The best way to find out was to stay close to Olivia, win her trust, get her to open up to him.

But he absolutely couldn't let down his guard and allow her to trap him with her sultry eyes and her real or *pretended* innocence.

THE NEXT MORNING, Olivia awakened from a restless sleep to her cell phone jangling. "Hello."

She'd expected it to be her boss, but a low voice echoed back. "I warned you. Now it's too late."

She sat up, triggering a sharp pain to slice through her shoulder. "Who is this?"

"Goodbye, Olivia."

The phone clicked into silence, the dial tone droning with the reminder of the eerie message. The voice had belonged to the man at the hospital. The one who'd taken her to the morgue. Did he know she was staying here with Craig?

She punched star sixty-nine but, as she'd expected, the call was unidentifiable. Probably a throwaway cell.

She shivered in spite of the heat, then pushed to her feet. The shower water was running in the bathroom and Craig would be out soon.

She wasn't alone.

A minute later, Craig appeared with a towel knotted around his waist. He took one look at her and frowned. "What's wrong?"

Olivia had never relied on anyone else, but she and Craig had to work together. "I just received another call."

A cold mask flew over his face. "What did he say?"

"That he'd already warned me once." She licked her dry lips, wishing he'd said more, that she could have kept him on the phone longer. "That it was too late."

"Too late?" He moved toward her, gripped her arms. "Too late for what?"

"I don't know." A shiver chased up her spine. "He didn't say. He just hung up. I tried star sixty-nine but it didn't work. He's probably using a throwaway cell."

"Probably. We have to get a tracer on your phone." Craig reached out and feathered a strand of hair from her face. "I don't like him using you, Olivia."

Olivia shrugged. "I just want us to find out what's going on."

Craig nodded, then studied her for a minute. "Thank you for telling me. It's important we trust each other."

She twisted her hands together. She wanted to trust him. But trust didn't come easy. Not with her job or her personal life. And she knew it didn't come easy with Craig, either.

"I'm going to CIRP this morning," he finally said.

"I'll be ready in a minute."

He nodded, then glanced at her shoulder. "Do you need help?"

Yes, she did. She suddenly wanted him to make all this go away. To undress her and carry through on the promise of heat she'd seen in his eyes the night before. "No. I'm fine."

"I'll have coffee and breakfast ready by the time you're dressed."

He gave her an odd look, making her wonder about the other females in his life. Did he have a girlfriend somewhere who would question why Olivia was staying at his place? He'd made no mention of a lover. And she hadn't seen any signs of a woman in his house or bathroom. Not even an extra toothbrush.

Why did Craig keep himself so bottled up and restrained? Why didn't he have a lover?

He stopped at the small corner desk, stuffed a folder inside it, snapped it shut, then strode into the kitchen. She shook off her troubling thoughts and rushed to the bathroom, struggling with the sling and her clothes as she tried to freshen up. The sound of the caller's voice haunted her as she faced herself in the mirror and brushed on powder to hide the dark circles beneath her eyes.

The wound on her shoulder was a visible reminder of the danger dogging her, and the fact that her father's body lay dead in the morgue, the virus that had killed him still unknown.

OLIVIA MIGHT CLAIM she didn't need anyone, but the hardheaded woman was a walking nightmare. She was still weak, yet she'd ignored his eggs and toast for a couple of truffles with her coffee on the way out the door. She was stubborn, opinionated, tenacious and practically bohemian in her lifestyle, ignoring her personal needs for her job.

He grimaced, realizing that, except for the eating habits, he'd described himself. And that instead of being turned off by those characteristics, they drew him to her like a ship in the darkness to a beacon of light. She was so unlike his own mother, who, though she was a virtual pillar by his father's side, was unable to make a decision for herself or voice her own thoughts. His mom needed parties and doting attention and to be in the limelight, whereas Olivia needed to make things happen, would stand up for a cause she believed in and wouldn't give up without a fight.

The scent of her skin teased him with other *what-ifs* as they drove to CIRP. What if they could forget the case? Go back to his place and make love all day? What if he could forget she was a reporter?

But he couldn't.

And he shouldn't feel guilty for looking into her past. He'd had every right to research her the night before.

Her father had died. And for all he knew, she could be a plant sent to seduce him long enough to sidetrack him from finding the truth. Invading a person's privacy came with the job. It had never bothered him before. He didn't like that it did now.

They met with Ian Hall first, then were escorted to the office of Thornbird's co-worker, Dr. Fred Fulton.

He and Olivia both claimed chairs opposite Fulton's desk. Fulton was polished, well-spoken, and wore a suit and tie, far from the geeky madman-scientist look that Thornbird had captured so well. Except for a notable limp and the cigar box on his credenza which indicated he smoked, he appeared to be fit. The only distinguishing feature was his handlebar mustache, but it was also neat and suited the man.

"You worked with my father on this virus?" Olivia asked.

"Yes, Miss Thornbird. My condolences." He crossed his legs, resting his hand on his leg, twirling the cigar between his thumb and fingers. "Your father was a genius. It's our loss that he's gone."

Olivia nodded, although a small flinch betrayed her bravado.

"What can you tell us about the virus?" Craig asked.

"It attacks the amygdala part of the brain just under the cerebral cortex. Stimulation of the amygdaloid nuclei control different patterns of behavior. Later, it begins attacking the central nervous system, causes fever and the rash. Eventually, the body shuts down."

"So, the physical reaction in the brain triggers psychosis?"

He nodded. "Patients begin hearing voices, may experience ringing in their ears, their thought patterns become jumbled. Often they see patterns and may even hallucinate."

"How long from being infected until the symptoms appear?"

"The virus appears to attack suddenly. But we can't be certain. It would help if we knew exactly how the victims are infected, the exact time. Then we could determine specifics."

"Have you seen anything like this before?"

Fulton pulled at his craggy chin. "A few years ago, we thought the Germans might have created a similar virus, but it was supposedly destroyed."

"Was that the virus that killed my mother?" Olivia asked.

Fulton inhaled, then blew out smoke. "I…don't know. Your mother's death was unfortunate, though."

Craig shifted in his seat. "Do you know of any terrorist cells seeking germs from the U.S.?"

"No, but I'm sure there are some," Dr. Fulton said.

Craig nodded. "Thanks. If you think of anything else, call me."

Dr. Fulton stood. "Believe me, Agent Horn, I want to isolate this germ and find out how it's spreading so we can stop it. If it's fallen into the wrong hands, this series of suicides may only be a hint of what's to come."

Craig grabbed a business card with the doctor's number, then he and Olivia left in silence.

"I'd like to look at those old files," Olivia said. "The virus he referred to—maybe it's a mutated strain from the one that killed my mother. The government covered it up back then, and CIRP might have information on it now."

"Do you know where old records would be kept?"

"If they kept them, they'd be in the basement." Olivia motioned for him to follow. "Come on, there's a service elevator we can take to bypass security."

Craig followed, checking over their shoulders to make sure they didn't get caught.

SPECIAL AGENT CRAIG HORN and Olivia Thornbird were taking the service elevator to the basement.

He gripped his hands, the numerous scars reddening beneath the patterns of the overhead light as he disappeared into the shadows to retrieve his tools. The elevator would malfunction. A simple little rewiring job would do the trick.

Moving silently, he strode to the shaft to loosen the bolts and screws. The janitor's uniform had certainly come in handy. Too bad the guy who'd been wearing it hadn't wanted to give it up.

A rumble of laughter caught in his throat. The chump had died for a stupid uniform. Had clung to it as if the coveralls meant he was someone important.

But he knew better. Important meant holding people's lives in your hand. Controlling them. Planning for the future. Having the ultimate power over life and death.

No one knew better than him the importance of protecting citizens. So, a few died in the process. It was the greater good of the people as a whole that mattered.

Senator Horn's words, exactly.

He crawled inside the elevator shaft and began to work. Agent Horn and Olivia Thornbird wanted to go to the basement. They would definitely make it there, a lot sooner than they expected.

And it would be the ride of their lifetimes—their very last, to be exact.

Yes, Olivia Thornbird's nine lives had finally run out. The shooting. The chocolates. The elevator.

One way or the other, she would die. And this time, she'd take Agent Horn with her.

Chapter Eleven

Excitement strummed through Olivia at the prospect of finding new information about her mother's death, but the grinding of the elevator jarred the pain in her arm.

"Olivia, I spoke to the medical examiner this morning while you were getting dressed." Craig's voice rumbled with the vibration of the elevator's descent. "He hopes to release your father's body tomorrow, so if you want to start making funeral arrangements, you can."

She gripped the metal edge for support, a series of images flashing before her. Her father's dead body. The casket. Saying goodbye.

She wished she could bury him next to her mother so they could rest in peace together. But her mother's cremation meant she didn't even have a grave to visit.

Suddenly the elevator jerked to a stop between floors. Craig frowned and pushed the Open Door button, but the door refused to budge. Then the floor shook, a screeching sound erupted from the sides and walls, and the elevator careened downward at an accelerated speed.

Olivia screamed and stumbled sideways to regain her balance. Craig grabbed her to steady her, his expression alarmed as he punched the Emergency button. Instead of slowing, the elevator increased its speed. Craig pressed the Emergency button again and an alarm wailed, but abruptly ended as quickly as it had sounded.

"Hang on!" Craig cradled her against him, pulling them to the floor, then covered her head with his body to protect her as they plunged downward.

Seconds later, the elevator slammed to a halt. Metal ground and sparks flew in all directions. The impact threw them both against the sides of the elevator with such force that Olivia's head hit the wall and dark spots danced before her eyes. A sharp ringing reverberated through her ears, and she crouched against Craig. The ringing continued inside her head—sharp, brittle, relentless.

The lights suddenly flickered off, and darkness swallowed the interior.

CRAIG GRIMACED AND SWIPED at the blood where he'd bitten his tongue, then struggled to sit up. It was so damn dark he couldn't see, and an odd odor, like burning rubber, seeped through the cramped space.

"Olivia?" He felt for her, lifted her gently from his side to check her over, careful of her wound. "Are you all right?"

"I...think so. Are you?"

"Yeah." Her voice sounded weak though, almost muffled, as if she was disoriented. "Did you hit your head?"

"Yes, but it's all right." She twisted against him in the dark, the close contact nearly his undoing. They'd almost died seconds ago, and all he had thought about was holding on to her. Making sure she was safe.

Somewhere in those frantic thoughts, he'd realized

how much he wanted to make love to her. That nothing mattered except making certain she was still alive so he could taste her one more time.

"I…how long do you think we'll be here?" Olivia asked, a faint panicked note in her tone.

"I don't know. The alarm went off so someone should try to rescue us."

"Unless they don't want us found."

Craig tightened his hold around her. The alarm had ended so abruptly he'd wondered himself.

The air swirled with smoky remnants of the fall, their breaths the only sound in the tension-filled minute that stretched between them.

"I'm sorry I dragged you and your father into all this, Olivia."

Her hands slid up to cover his. He hadn't realized he was gripping her face between his palms, that he'd moved so close their bodies brushed until he felt her breasts pushing against his chest.

"You just did your job," she said softly.

He swallowed hard. She'd almost been killed three times, twice while under his care. He didn't know if the killer was personally trying to flaunt his skill in Craig's face, but he didn't like the guy's methods or his unflappable gall.

He'd also underestimated Craig. By trying to kill Olivia while she was in Craig's custody, the SOB had made the game personal.

And Craig would die before he'd let him hurt her again.

OLIVIA DIDN'T UNDERSTAND the anger in Craig's tone, but as his hand traced her face, the realization that once again she could have died assaulted her. She was only twenty-three. She didn't want to die. She had so much to live for. Her work. Her…family?

No, no family. No boyfriend or lover. Not a soul who would care if she met her demise.

Terror-stricken at the thought, she burrowed deeper against Craig. The cold steel walls of the elevator closed around her, the darkness sending a tingle along her neck as if icy fingers were clawing at her skin. A small voice echoed inside her head, whispering that someone wanted her dead. Or maybe there was more than one person.

They're coming for you. Just like they did for your mother and father, and the others.

A strangled cry escaped her. The ringing in her ears faded slightly, then dulled to an eerie drone as if her eardrum might have ruptured.

"Olivia?" Craig stroked the hair from her cheek. "What's wrong?"

She clutched his hand, savoring the feel of his touch on her skin as she composed herself. "I…I don't know. I guess it's all been too much."

Her soft admission seemed to unravel the layers of apprehension between them. Except another kind of tension that had been brewing between them erupted, and he dragged her into his arms. Once his lips touched hers, she was lost in the fiery sensations that spiraled through her. He teased her lips apart with his tongue, probed the deep recesses of her mouth, tasting, exploring, weaving a delicious hunger inside her with his tormenting strokes. His hands massaged her back, tickled her neck, then skimmed lower to rub the indentation of her spine before trailing around her waist to the under-side of her breasts.

"Olivia." His breath rasped out as he deepened the kiss, then lifted one hand to cup the weight of her in his palm. He threw his leg over hers, entwining their bod-ies and pulling her so close she felt the heady rise and fall of his chest. Masculine muscles pulsed and tensed as he caressed her back, the corded muscles in his arms bulging as he gripped her closer.

Dizzy, she moaned, deep and throaty, curling deeper into his embrace as she met his tongue with her own. They danced the mating dance, sipping and kissing until he dropped his head to her neck and trailed more kisses along the tender skin of her nape. Her nipples grew hard, her body steeping with heat, the pool of desire growing so hot within her it was raging out of control. He inched his fingers beneath her shirt, shifted the lace of her bra so that her breasts spilled over into his hungry waiting hands. Then he traced his fingers over her nipple, bring-ing it to a turgid aching peak before he dropped his head, groaned and took her nipple into his mouth.

A deep yearning burst open within her as he suckled her, a need so all-consuming it begged to be released from its imprisonment. She'd been alone all her life. Working. Drifting through each day, detached.

Because becoming involved meant getting hurt. Being left behind.

But this time, she wouldn't get emotional. She sim-ply needed comfort, assurance that she was still alive.

At least for the night.

"Olivia?"

She pulled back, heard the hesitation in his voice,

knew she should be questioning this herself. But they were lost in this dark world, separated from everything for the moment. And for some reason, she found herself not wanting to be rescued.

Not just yet.

So she slowly reached up and began to loosen his tie. One flick. Two. The knot slipped loose. Then came his buttons. Finally she felt the thick hair on his chest, ran her fingers through the coarseness, stroked the corded muscles that hardened with his indrawn breath. Then she let her hand trail lower to tease his sex, the feel of his hard erection in her hand driving her wild with desire.

OLIVIA LOVED THE SAME WAY she worked, with intensity and gusto and spice. Craig forced her hand away, afraid he might lose it before he gave her pleasure. And her pleasure seemed to be uppermost in his mind.

Forget work. The case. That her father might have been responsible for ending so many lives.

That the two of them had almost died.

All that mattered was being inside her, making them both feel alive.

He inhaled, struggling to control his raging desires, but the odd odor he'd sniffed earlier permeated the air. Suddenly cognizant that that burning smell originated from the elevator malfunction, that the odor indicated more trouble, he eased away from her and stood, abruptly yanking his shirt together as he tried to adjust his eyes and scan the darkness. He had to get help. Get them out before they died.

"Craig?"

Her voice sounded lost, small in the darkness that swallowed them. Hurt. Confused.

"We have to get out of here."

"I know, but…"

He gripped her hands when she reached for him. "Olivia, I smell fire."

His crisply delivered words jerked her into the present. She pushed to her feet, holding on to him to gain her balance. He was suddenly grateful she was so resilient and tough. She would need that strength if they were going to escape alive.

"Where's it coming from?"

"My guess is below us, but I can't be sure."

She dug her nail into his arms. "What do we do?"

"Try the Emergency button again. I'll see if I can find a way out of here."

She did, to no avail, then ran her fingers over the wall in search of an emergency phone. When she found it, it wasn't working, so she fumbled for her cell phone and dialed frantically.

"There's no service."

He tossed her his phone. "Try mine."

While she felt for the numbers, he removed his tie and swung it upward to catch on an exposed bar across the ceiling. It took him three times, but he finally snagged the beam. Then he used it to help him scale the wall. The tie ripped just before he grabbed the beam, but he managed to leap and get one hand around the metal tubing.

"Craig, your cell isn't working, either."

He hated the panic in her voice. "It's all right. I might be able to get us to a vent and we can crawl out."

"What are you doing?"

"Removing the ceiling panel." He fumbled with his pocketknife, felt with his loose hand for the screws bolting the panel into place, then slowly worked one free.

Olivia's breath hissed through the air. "Why hasn't someone rescued us by now? There should have been an emergency alarm."

Craig cursed, struggling with the second bolt. "My guess is someone rigged the elevator so it would fall. They probably dismantled the alarm as well."

Olivia gasped. "Then we must be really on to something," Olivia said. "Or else why would someone want us dead?"

"Right." Craig cursed again. If he didn't get the bolts loose, the bastard was going to succeed. The carbon monoxide was slowly seeping into the elevator. He could already feel himself getting woozy.

"Cover your mouth and nose," he shouted. "Try not to breathe in."

Olivia hunkered down low, pulled her shirt up over her face and did as he said. It would have been a priceless moment if he hadn't been so scared that they were going to die.

THE SLIGHT RINGING had started again in Olivia's head. Or maybe it was just the panic.

You're going to die. It won't be long now until they get you just like they did your father.

No...

"Olivia?"

She wrapped her uninjured arm around her knee, then glanced up. Through the murky shadows, she realized that Craig had nearly unbolted the ceiling panel. A tiny sliver of light flowed through the opening. The screech of his pocketknife in the metal splintered the air, and the screw clattered to the floor.

"I'll check it out, then come back for you."

Don't go. She stifled the plea and nodded, although she knew he couldn't see her in the dark.

Seconds lapsed into forever as he hurdled himself into the shaft. The odd smell grew stronger, the faint scent of smoke mingling with the odor.

Craig shouted her name. "Let me help you up. We're between floors, but there's a vent we can crawl through."

She stood and hurried to the opening, but even stretched on tiptoe, she couldn't reach his extended arm.

"Come on, Olivia. We need to hurry."

"I can't make it. You go ahead. Get help."

"I'm not leaving without you," he growled.

"But I can't reach you."

He dropped to the floor, gripped her arms and forced her to look at him. "Listen to me. You're the toughest woman I know. Trust me. You can do this. We have to hurry."

She did trust him. More than she ever had another man. But she couldn't climb into that well of darkness. The shadows, the voices were amplified; the hot air was suffocating. Her breathing grew unsteady, and she trembled in his arms.

He shook her gently. "Come on, I'll hoist you up. I know it'll be hard to hang on with one hand, but I'll climb up and pull you the rest of the way."

He bent and kissed her one more time, then stooped to lift her. Olivia licked her lips and reached up to grab the metal rod. Her body shook as she wrapped her fingers along the metal pipe. Craig made a running leap, scaled two steps up the wall and grabbed the pole, then hurled himself up into the shaft. Seconds later, he lay on his belly with his hand clamped over her wrist. Her hand was slippery, starting to slide...

"Go ahead, let go, I have you," he said in a strained voice.

She heard the encouragement and determination in his voice and released her grip long enough to fumble for his hand. She screamed, almost slipping, but he encircled her wrist with both of his hands. Her arm felt as if it were being wrenched from the socket as he dragged her up. She fell into the small landing with him, her breath gushing out. He braced her head against him for a brief second, soothing her nerves.

The odor grew stronger, more pungent. Heat seared her skin and smoke billowed into the elevator shaft.

"You okay?"

She nodded and pushed up. "Yeah, let's get out of here."

He brushed her shoulder as she pivoted and crawled through the narrow opening. Darkness consumed her as she plunged into the space to follow him, the sound of Craig's breathing a lifeline in the darkness.

Just as they made it to the end and Craig pushed open the vent, the elevator exploded below them. A ball of fire surged up where they had just been, smoke streaming through the vent. Flames licked at her feet as she dropped onto the floor beside Craig. Another fireball careened through the vent toward them. Sparks flew and hissed, and another explosion rocked the building as they sprinted away.

Chapter Twelve

Chaos reigned for the next half hour. The fire alarm sounded through the halls; a constant barrage of intermittent warnings blared over the intercom, ordering everyone to evacuate.

Craig pulled Olivia along beside him as they ran down the steps to safety. The fire truck roared up toward the building, a steady stream of doctors, scientists and other employees of CIRP flooding the lawn. A few had managed to snag laptops and briefcases and clutched them to their sides as if to guard the contents.

Hushed whispers, worried voices and shrieks sprang out as smoke poured through one of the doors. "What's going on?"

"Where did the fire start?"

"I heard the service elevator exploded!"

"Is everyone out?"

"I wish I'd grabbed my computer."

Craig whirled Olivia around to face him, his heart pounding. "Are you okay?"

She nodded, although her eyes were glassy, and she was coughing. "Those files."

"May be the reason for the fire."

Olivia gasped. "You mean you think someone did this to stop *us?*"

He shrugged, perspiration trickling down his neck into the collar of his shirt. "I don't know, but I damn sure intend to find out." The fact that Olivia had almost died three times in two days wasn't a coincidence. He hauled her up next to him while his gaze scanned the property, searching for anyone among the crowd who looked suspicious. If someone had set the fire to kill them, he might be waiting outside, watching to see if they escaped alive.

Two more fire trucks arrived, the firemen jumping into motion. CIRP's security, Seaside Securities, combed the area, checking to make sure everyone was safe.

Craig spotted Ian Hall in a heated conversation with Dr. Fulton and headed toward him. Olivia followed and Hall spun toward them, his expression grim.

"I was just asking Dr. Fulton if you two made it out all right."

"We got stuck in an elevator that nearly plunged us to our deaths," Craig snapped. "If I hadn't unbolted the top panel so we could crawl through the vent, we'd both be trapped inside right now. Dead."

Hall's face blanched while Fulton staggered back, pulling at his mustache. "My God, you aren't suggesting that someone intentionally set that fire?"

"That's exactly what I'm suggesting." Craig stabbed a finger at Hall. "Which makes it obvious that someone here doesn't want me asking questions. What are you hiding, Dr. Hall?"

He bristled and adjusted his suit jacket. "I resent

your implications. I've cooperated with you and the local police fully. Dr. Fulton is even trying to pinpoint the nature of this virus to help you." Craig started to argue, but Hall continued, "I'll speak to the fire chief now and my security, and get to the bottom of what caused this fire."

"I want to know what you find out," Craig said between gritted teeth.

Hall gave a clipped nod. "I'll have the fire chief's report sent to you as soon as he completes his investigation."

"I'll be expecting it." Still, Craig silently cursed as Hall walked off. He just hoped to hell the firemen contained the fire so Fulton's research wouldn't be lost.

THE SEA OF FACES swam in front of Olivia in a dizzying frenzy. White lab coats. Nurses. Technicians. Firemen.

Concerned people who were just trying to do their jobs had been put in danger.

Why? Because she and Craig were asking questions.

Anger churned through her. Whoever had tried to kill her wanted to so badly that he'd risked getting caught to do it. And he'd put all these other lives in jeopardy, too.

"I don't understand, Craig. Why endanger all these other people and the scientists' valuable work just to hurt me?"

He dotted his face with his handkerchief. Then he gently reached up and wiped at her cheek. "You have black soot there," he said in a low voice. Her gaze met his, tension thrumming between them. "Whoever wants you thinks it's worth the risk."

She gripped his hands, that faint ringing echoing in her head again. "They must think I know more than I do."

The brief flicker of suspicion in his eyes cut her to the bone.

"Craig, you don't think I'm keeping something from you, do you?"

His mouth flattened into a thin cold line. "You didn't tell me about that phone call at first."

She gripped him tighter, ignoring the pandemonium surrounding them. It was suddenly very important to her that he believe her. "I explained that. And I'm not here to get information on your family like that other reporter, I'm just trying to find the truth about my parents' deaths." She gestured toward the crowd, her heart in her throat. "I would never jeopardize these people's lives. That's the reason I chased the story about my mother, and now my dad. I don't want the truth about what happened to them buried, or information about some dangerous virus kept from the public if citizens can protect themselves."

Something dark shifted in his eyes. "Then we have to figure out what they think you know."

Her heart fluttered in relief. So, he did believe her.

Yet at the same time, her mind raced for answers. And a sense of fear overwhelmed her. She felt as if someone was watching her. Searching her out through the crowd. She glanced through the throng of people, dissecting faces, wondering if the lab coats and phony smiles were a mere disguise for what lay below the surface.

"Olivia?"

She spotted a tall muscular man fading into the background. He had beady eyes. Now she remembered… more details.

She started forward, had to find him.

"Olivia, what's wrong?"

"I...thought I saw the man who tried to kill me at the hospital. He had dark eyes and a mole on his chin."

Craig instantly removed his gun and glanced into the crowd. "Where?"

She pointed past a group of employees to the sea oats and wooded area beyond. Behind it, the jagged edges of a cliff overlooked the ocean. "Over there."

Craig grabbed her hand and dragged her through the crowd. "Tell me if you spot him again. What was he wearing?"

"A lab coat. And maybe scrubs." Her gaze swung left and right, her head spinning as she searched the throng. But everyone blended together. Suddenly every face possessed those same intensely evil eyes.

Craig halted at a clearing of brush, pointed toward the cliffs that bordered the property. Dark clouds gave the sky a sinister grayness. Shadows soared above the ocean from the ridges like bony skeletons ready to grab her.

She could barely see beyond her own hand. Except somehow she knew those beady eyes were watching her. She could almost smell the scent of blood and sweat on the killer. The scent of death.

"I'll search the cliffs," Craig said. "You go back to the crowd."

"No." Panic tightened her chest as she tugged at his hand. The killer's face loomed behind every man. "Don't leave me, Craig."

"But this might be our chance to catch him."

"It's too dark," she argued. "If he was there, he's long gone."

Craig frowned. "You're sure you saw him, though?"

The faces swam in front of her, each one peering at her, each one more menacing, as if they'd risen from the grave. The image of a needle in the man's hand rose through the mist. "I...I'm not sure."

He stroked her arm, his voice low and throaty. "Olivia, did you recognize him?"

"I don't know. I..." Her voice broke. "I...thought I saw his eyes, but I didn't see his face that day. Except for a second. He had a small mole on his chin." And now everyone looked like a killer.

The voices started again. *I'm coming for you, Olivia. You're going to die.*

The incessant ringing followed. The shrill sound of her father's gunshot. Her own cry.

She covered her ears with her hands to drown out the sounds. God, what was happening to her? Was she losing her mind?

"Olivia?"

Craig's voice sounded as if it were a million miles away, lost in a wind tunnel.

"Olivia, are you all right?"

She nodded, although she wasn't all right at all. A killer wanted her. She had to know why.

Emotions she didn't like, and refused to acknowledge, surfaced. Fear. Dread. A sense of evil. A desperate need to burrow herself into Craig's protective embrace. "Maybe whoever did this thinks my father told me about his work."

Craig's frown deepened. "He didn't give you a journal, maybe a file?"

Olivia shook her head. "No, but maybe he left one in the house somewhere."

"We didn't find anything before. And we're still trying to decipher his confidential files," Craig said. "I'll call and see if the house has been released, and we'll check it one more time."

She nodded. The wind howled off the cliffs, and the cries of the suicide victims floated in with the tide. As if she were looking at a movie screen, Olivia suddenly saw herself hurtling off one of the cliffs, falling, falling, falling, saying her final goodbye.

As THEY LEFT CIRP, Craig phoned Agent Devlin and played catch-up.

"We must be getting close," Agent Devlin said. "I heard from the CDC and Oberman. The vics' homes are clear. The virus is not transmitted through air vents or structural faults, and no bacteria appears to have been absorbed into any structural materials. They also don't think it's contagious or that it spreads through physical contact."

"That's a relief," Craig said. "Although the victims have to be contracting it from somewhere. Did the mail check out?"

"So far, it's clean," Devlin said.

Craig gritted his teeth in frustration. "We're on our way to Thornbird's house. The killer obviously thinks Olivia is a threat, so we're going to see if we missed something before."

"It's worth a shot." Devlin sighed. "I've made some contacts here. A German named Iska Milaski has been known for experimenting with germ warfare. We're trying to locate him now." He hesitated. "Another name cropped up in conjunction with Dr. Thornbird, too. Dr. Martin Shubert."

"He worked with Olivia's father?"

"No, her mother."

Craig steered around a Ford pickup and glanced at Olivia. She was resting her head against the seat. Her cheeks looked so white, her dainty pink lips parted slightly, her stubborn chin relaxed.

He almost reached out and covered her hand with his own, but he jerked his attention back to the case. "What's the story?"

"Shubert used to travel internationally," Devlin said. "But he retired several years ago. And he's not far from Savannah. Lives on Tybee Island."

"Interesting. Any more information?"

"Feel Olivia out, see if she recognizes the name. Then pay him a visit. He may be our missing link in this whole case." Devlin recited the address.

"I'm on it. Let me know if you find Milaski."

Devlin agreed and hung up, then Craig phoned to confirm that the house was cleared. Craig maneuvered through traffic to Olivia's father's house, then parked in the drive and slanted a look toward Olivia. When they'd been trapped in that elevator, he'd nearly made love to her. Had felt the hurt and fear in her touch and it had driven him wild. And when she'd told him she wouldn't hurt anyone, he'd believed her. Had almost trusted her.

Olivia shifted, then opened her eyes. In spite of fatigue lines and the exhaustion from their earlier ordeal, she was still beautiful. Her long blond hair spilled around her shoulders in a tangle, her lips were parted slightly, giving her that sultry but innocent look that enticed him to forget all the reasons he'd sworn not to get involved with her. She looked like an angel when she was sleeping, a seductress when she smiled.

Hell, he still wanted her. Wanted her so bad he ached.

But was the angel part simply a disguise?

OLIVIA SAT UP and massaged her temple. Her head throbbed as badly as her shoulder, but thankfully the ringing had subsided slightly. "Who was on the phone?"

A frown knitted his brows. "Agent Devlin. He had a couple of names he wanted to run by me." Craig's gaze grew more intense. "A German named Iska Milaski. Rumor has it he'd been working on germ warfare."

Olivia exhaled slowly. "Does Devlin know where he is?"

"No, but they're looking. Have you heard of him?"

Olivia searched her memory banks. "No. Who was the other one?"

"Dr. Martin Shubert."

Shubert? The name from the file she'd seen in her father's computer.

"Olivia, do you know him?"

Craig's tone sounded almost accusatory. She scrunched her face, the pounding in her head intensifying. "No, but his name was in one of my father's files on his computer at CIRP."

"So you kept it from me?"

"I'm sorry, I wasn't sure if it meant anything or not."

His pause reverberated with more doubt. "What was his name in reference to?"

"My mother." The well of grief inside her opened up, threatening to swallow her again. "I found it the day I got caught in my father's office, but the guards dragged me away before I could read anything on him."

"The day you were shot?"

"Yes. And when I looked him up online, I couldn't find anything." A shiver chased down her spine. "What does Agent Devlin know about him?"

"Not much. But he gave me an address on Tybee Island where Shubert retired. Once we check your father's house again, we'll pay him a visit."

Olivia reached for the door handle. "Then let's stop wasting time."

The sight of the cordoned-off house and warning signs registered in the back of her mind as she entered. Craig followed her inside, his gaze running over the small den. "I'll check in here again, then in the basement."

Olivia nodded. "I'll start in his bedroom."

She hurried to his room, ignoring the stab of nostalgia that assaulted her at the sight of her father's bed, the chair in the corner that held discarded lab coats, the clothes in his closet that he would never again wear. The scent of Old Spice…

The room felt stifling hot, the pain in her shoulder a constant drumming ache as she rummaged through each of his pants pockets, shirts and jackets. Next, she searched the dresser drawers, the nightstand, the bathroom. She wasn't sure what she was looking for—maybe a date book, journal, computer disk, notepad…

A half hour later, she gave up and went to the kitchen. Craig had finished in the den and had retreated to the basement. He'd seemed disturbed when he'd hung up on Agent Devlin. Had he learned new information he didn't want to share?

Worry knotted her stomach as she combed through drawers, but the kitchen turned up empty, too. Frustrated, she walked to the den and picked up the photograph of her mother sitting on the end table. Her mother's smile captivated her, the old-fashioned dress still beautiful on her slim figure. She'd never been much for makeup. Only a simple strand of pearls circled her neck; matching earrings in her lobes twinkled in the dim light flickering from the lamp.

These will be yours someday, Livvy.

The choking grief rushed back. She remembered that day so clearly. On her fifth birthday, her mother had given her a box filled with costume jewelry. Then she'd fingered the strand of pearls around her neck.

"One day, you'll be a big girl. Then Mommy will let you wear her real pearls."

Where were the necklace and earrings?

Suddenly anxious, she mentally reviewed the contents of her father's bedroom. Her mother's things had been packed and stored, taken to the attic years ago.

Her pulse raced. She had to check the attic. If her father wanted to hide something, he might have hidden it up there. Spurred by adrenaline, she drew down the ladder, then climbed into the musty room. Dust and cobwebs clung to the wood, the scent of cedar and age filling the air. She spotted an old trunk and rushed to it, more emotions surfacing as she discovered her mother's clothes packed inside.

She dug through the chest, and found a red dress she remembered from one Christmas, a pair of high heels she'd played dress-up in, a hat her mother had worn one Easter, then a box of her own childhood drawings, pictures she'd made for her mother. Her throat clogged as the memories flooded her, and she dug deeper and unearthed a small jewelry box tucked underneath the layers of clothes. Inside, the pearl necklace and earrings lay on a bed of ivory satin. She lifted the strand of pearls gingerly, brushed the smooth glossy white globes against her cheek and saw her mother's face in her mind. Then something slipped from the box.

A computer diskette.

"Olivia?"

She jammed the diskette inside her jeans, then stood and met Craig at the attic entrance.

"Did you find anything?" Craig asked.

She hesitated, contemplating whether to show him the disk. But a moment of paranoia hit her and she held back. "No. Nothing."

But the diskette burned a hole in her pocket at her lie.

DISAPPOINTED THAT THEY HADN'T found anything at Thornbird's again, Craig drove toward Shubert's hoping for better luck. Olivia seemed distracted, worried, quiet. Then again, it had been a hell of a day, and she hadn't yet recovered from her gunshot wound or her grief. A weaker woman would have already fallen apart.

Admiration for her stirred again, as well as that strong sexual pull, but he tamped it down as they parked at the house where Shubert lived. The two-story Georgian structure stood out among the other summer cottages. Giant azaleas, colorful flower beds and live oaks dripping with Spanish moss added an ambience to the estate lot. For a scientist, Shubert seemed to have done well financially.

Olivia followed him up to the door in silence, the anticipation as thick as the oppressive heat that made his shirt cling to his back. He rang the doorbell and tapped his foot impatiently, shooing away a gnat as they waited while Olivia's breath rattled in the quiet.

A few seconds later, a short balding man wearing a butler's uniform opened the door, exposing a two-story foyer decorated in an almost garish oriental style.

"We're here to see Dr. Martin Shubert," Craig said. He flashed his badge. "Special Agent Craig Horn, FBI."

The little man's eye twitched. "Excuse me, sir, but what is this about?"

"A case," Craig said without elaborating as he pushed his way inside. "Please get Dr. Shubert."

The butler's nervous gaze flickered over Craig, then Olivia. "Dr. Shubert isn't feeling well, sir. I don't think—"

"I have to speak to him," Craig said, refusing to be brushed off. "Now, either ask him to come down here or take us to him."

"I…I don't think he's going to be of much help." The butler coughed into his hand. "You don't understand—"

"No, you don't understand," Craig snapped. "I will talk to him. And if he doesn't cooperate, I have the power to arrest him."

This time, the little man's bald head glowed red with anger. "Very well. Follow me."

Offering a clipped military turn, he led the way up the winding staircase. Craig's gaze swept his surroundings. The lurid artwork flanking the walls and flashy red-and-gold accents clashed with the stately manor of the house's exterior.

"He's retired for the night," the butler said as he opened the room to a massive bedroom suite. Plush white carpet embraced heavy dark furniture to form a sitting area that joined the master bedroom. Heavy velvet drapes were drawn shut, blocking out the woods beyond, a small lamp in the corner the only source of light in a room weighted with a sense of desolation.

Olivia gave Craig an odd look as the butler stepped away, her unease mirroring Craig's. A shrunken man lay on the bed enfolded in a heavy silk comforter. Dozens of pillows at the headboard propped him to a half-sitting position, although his head had fallen sideways, spittle dribbling from his chin.

"Dr. Shubert?"

The man didn't respond, although his eyelids fluttered open as if he realized someone had entered the room. Craig stepped closer, his instincts alert.

"Dr. Shubert, my name is Craig Horn. I'm with the FBI."

Shubert's eyes appeared glazed, his wrinkled face thick with age lines, his gnarled hand jerking as he clutched the sheet between fingers that were milky white.

Craig cleared his throat, directing his comment to the butler. "What's wrong with him?"

The butler lay a comforting hand on Shubert's shoulder to soothe him. Then Shubert's eyes closed again as if he were drifting to sleep.

"I tried to tell you. He's blind and deaf, and lives in constant pain. He's been ill for years, but his condition has deteriorated lately."

"What happened?" Craig asked.

"He contracted a rare virus while working overseas

years ago. The others who contracted it died, but by a miracle he managed to survive." The butler gestured toward the man's pathetic state. "Unfortunately, this is what it did to him."

"He can't communicate at all?" Olivia asked.

The butler shook his head. "He hasn't spoken in the ten years I've been with him."

Craig straightened his tie, his palms sweating. "I need the name of his doctor."

A sharp grunt was the butler's only reply. He motioned them to follow him downstairs, then located the information, scribbled it on a notepad and handed it to Craig.

Craig thanked him, and he and Olivia headed to the car.

"Do you think he had the same virus that killed my mother?" Olivia asked.

Craig shrugged. "Maybe this doctor and Shubert's medical files will tell us more."

An anguished look twisted Olivia's face as they climbed in the car. "He was the last hope I had for finding out what happened to my mother."

He squeezed her hand. "Don't give up, Olivia."

Dread filled Craig, along with more questions. If Shubert had been ill for years, he couldn't be responsible for the current rash of viruses in Savannah or the attacks on Olivia.

Which meant they still had no real leads, and that Olivia was still in danger…

NIGHT PAINTED SHADOWS around the interior of Craig's cabin as they entered. Silence stretched through the humid air, the buzzing of insects a backdrop to the apprehension tightening Olivia's muscles. They'd stopped and eaten a small meal at a diner, although Olivia's appetite had been minimal. Then she'd finally excused herself and showered. Anxious to see what was on the disk, she inserted it into her laptop and checked the menu, but the data appeared to be encrypted. Damn. She tried several passwords she thought her father might have used but came up with nothing.

She contemplated turning the diskette over to Craig, but paranoia still gripped her. Maybe she'd wait until she found out what kind of information the disk contained. After all, it might be nothing at all, or information on another project, one that was outdated and not related to the present. But if she found out it was important, she would give it to Craig.

Exhausted, she collapsed on top of Craig's bed. She should go home. Let him sleep in his own bed. Start acting independent again. But the frisson of fear that had dogged her the past few hours lingered, and she didn't want to leave the safety of his room.

Instead, she closed her eyes, yearning to have him near her. Holding her. Comforting her. Telling her everything was all right.

The desperate feeling was so unlike her that she wondered about her sanity.

Images of the elevator nearly plunging them to death, along with the following explosion, flashed back. On the heels of it, she saw Dr. Shubert's deteriorated body, then her mother's face. Had the two of them been infected by the same virus? If so, maybe death had actually spared her mother a long and painful debilitating disease.

But what did Shubert have to do with her father and this new strain of viruses? Maybe nothing…

Shivering, she burrowed beneath the covers, but other images assaulted her. Her father's bloody body. The other victims. The rash on their arms. The morgue.

Then the voices began again.

You're going to die, Olivia.

You're next.

She covered her ears, trying to drown out the sounds as she searched the darkness. But the onset of a panic attack threatened. Her lungs closed, and perspiration dotted her face and hands and neck. She wanted to run, to escape the shadows that plagued her, to shut out the voices.

But there was no place to run. No place that was safe for her to hide.

No place was safe for Olivia Thornbird. Except, once again, she'd escaped alive.

"I thought you were going to take care of them," his boss screamed into the telephone line.

He flexed his hands, stared at the burn scars, war wounds from his childhood given to him by the master to teach him how to be a man. His boss's beratement had once triggered insecurities. Fear.

No more.

He had learned control. "The woman should be feeling the symptoms by now. Give her a day or two, and she'll be contemplating ending her own life, that is *if* she already isn't."

"Was the stunt at CIRP really necessary? The feds already have the place under scrutiny, and God knows I want the Nighthawk Island facility to continue its work."

"You wanted the woman and agent dead. You didn't

specify where it had to take place." Memories of the fire rolling into the sky flashed in his mind, bringing a smile. The sight of the explosion today had done something to him. Made him almost randy. Given him a sense of power. "I did you a favor. The woman and agent were on their way to obtain records that you wouldn't have wanted found."

A long hesitation vibrated over the line. "True. But hell, Horn and Thornbird's daughter somehow found out about Shubert. They paid him a visit tonight."

"So? The old man is too far gone to tell them anything."

A fate also caused by his boss's manipulation and executed by him. He was what his boss had made him. Cold. Ruthless. Calculating.

And some sick sadistic rebellious part of him enjoyed hearing the sound of fear in his master's voice. An even deeper part wanted to torment his boss as he'd been tormented himself as a child.

But that wouldn't keep him from protecting the master with his life.

And taking others to please him.

Chapter Thirteen

Craig struggled with the urge to join Olivia in bed, his need for her so unsettling that he opened the French doors and breathed in the fresh air to clear his head. He stared into the moonless night as if the sky might offer him answers. Never had a woman driven such a wedge between him and his resolve to stay uninvolved.

But the sight of her hanging on for dear life in that elevator, then barely crawling from that vent alive replayed in his mind like a horror flick.

His cell phone jangled and he grabbed it, hoping it was Devlin with good news, a lead, anything to help solve this case. If he could just put some distance between himself and Olivia, he might be able to forget her. But he couldn't leave her alone with her life in jeopardy.

"Agent Horn."

"Craig, this is your father. What in heaven's name happened at CIRP today? I heard a news clip that you were in some kind of fire. I told you to make this suicide/virus case go away, not pull some theatrics and get that research park burned down."

His father was blaming him? Craig sighed and

dropped his head into his hands. He wanted to believe that his father cared, but his attitude hadn't changed. It never would. "Dad, I was at the research park to find answers that someone doesn't want found. Maybe you should change your focus to protecting the people instead of your own precious reputation."

A shocked sound reverberated back. "How dare you speak to me that way. I'm in politics because I'm representing the people. And what the hell were you doing at CIRP with a damn reporter? Didn't you learn the first time that you can't trust a journalist?"

"I don't need you to remind me of that debacle—"

"I've read Olivia Thornbird's articles," his father said, driving home his point. "She likes to stir up trouble, and she'll do anything she can to get a story just like—"

"She's not like that," Craig snapped.

His father cursed. "Don't tell me she already seduced you?"

Pain sliced through his knuckles as his fingers gripped the phone. "Who I sleep with or don't sleep with is none of your business." Furious at his father for being a jerk and at himself for letting his father make him feel like an adolescent, he slammed down the phone. How his mother tolerated playing second fiddle to a politician was beyond him. But she enjoyed being by his father's side, loved the public attention, liked being taken care of…

He would never allow politics or maintaining an image consume his life.

Except he had allowed his job to.

But that was a conscious choice. Knowing anyone who got close to him might be in danger was an excellent reason not to get close to Olivia or any other woman. Besides, he had to protect himself by not falling in love.

But was his father right about Olivia?

No…he didn't think so. She'd had every opportunity to seduce him, but she hadn't.

In fact, she seemed just as reluctant to complicate their relationship as he was. And she was nothing like his mother—hell, she balked at being taken care of.

The realization made him want her more.

A soft whimpering sound echoed from the bedroom, and he headed toward it. His pulse raced when he opened the door and saw Olivia's face and that golden hair fanned across the pillow, draping over one bare shoulder where her gown had slipped down. Instead of looking peaceful, though, she rolled into a fetal position in the throes of a nightmare. He walked to the bed, lowered himself beside her, then shook her gently. "Olivia?"

"No, don't, Daddy, don't die!" She twisted the sheet in her hands, her knuckles white. "Please help me, it's so dark…they're after me…"

He frowned and shook her again, gently brushed the hair from her face with his fingers. Her skin felt so warm to the touch, he wondered if she might have a fever. Worried, he pressed his palm to her forehead. It felt clammy. And her cheeks glowed pink in the dim light.

She suddenly flipped to her back, opened her eyes and gazed up at him.

"Olivia, it's okay," he said softly. "You must have been dreaming."

She nodded, her eyes big and frightened, dazed. Then she slipped one hand around his neck as if to pull him to her. Remembering their close call with death earlier, Craig gave in to the moment and cradled her against him. Careful of her injured shoulder, he soothed her with featherlight kisses. But those kisses heated his bloodstream, made the constant ache he had for her spiral out of control. Rational thought fled, replaced by primal instincts as the kisses soon grew hotter.

OLIVIA SHUT OUT the nightmares and voices, willing Craig's touch to make her whole again because in those dreams she had been falling apart. Fearing everybody and everything. Losing her independence and seeking refuge within the same four walls. She felt as if she were going crazy. Hot and cold at the same time. Her head swam with images of murder, pain, suicide.

Images of her father lying in a pool of blood. Her following...

Craig deepened the kiss, his hands skating over her shoulders, one tracing a path down her back, bringing her closer into the V of his thighs, and the nightmare dissipated slightly. His breath rasped between them as he pulled away and fingercombed the hair from her face. Then the heady sensation of his tongue warmed her insides as he claimed her mouth again. She threaded one hand in his thick hair, clinging to the muscles bunching in his arms as he held her. He was in great shape, but the suits and ties hid his physique, one she yearned to see more clearly. Hunger flowed within her, his own triggering her arousal to a fever pitch.

She reached for his tie, slid open the knot, dragged it from his neck and tossed it to the floor. Seconds later, she pushed his shirt away, raked her hands over the fine dusting of dark hair on his chest. And when she looked up into his eyes, the potent flare of heat drew her closer. He kissed her deeper, one hand snaking down to cover her breast and tease her nipple beneath her bra. Then he gently eased the buttons on her shirt free, trailed a path of kisses along her neck, then lower.

But the voices began again.

There's no place to hide, Olivia. You're the next to die.

She stiffened and pulled away, flattening her hands on his chest as she trembled with a combination of desire and fear.

"Olivia?" His voice sounded as if it had come from someone else.

"I…I've been fighting it, too, but this attraction…it's too strong." He implored her with his eyes, the heat flaring in the dark gray depths primal, without guard. The Iceman was gone, and in his place was a man determined to claim her. "I want you, Olivia."

Affection and admiration zinged inside her. She had known from the beginning that Craig was an honorable man. Strong. Brave. Intelligent.

A fierce competitor and agent.

But she'd underestimated his power as a man. His allure as a lover.

Still, the voices taunted her, perspiration beading on her neck and arms, shadows surrounding her. The walls were closing in again, the darkness hovering with the whisper of evil ready to pounce on her. She trembled again and glanced at the door, wanting to escape.

But she couldn't leave the house or she would die.

Olivia had never worried about being safe before.

The realization was even more jarring than the increasing reality that she was falling for Craig Horn.

The nightmares, the voices—what did they mean? The symptoms of the other victims resounded in her head. Paranoia. Hallucinations. Agoraphobia.

Illusions of suicide.

Dear God, could she possibly have contracted the virus herself?

CRAIG HAD NO IDEA why Olivia had pushed him away. He should be relieved that she possessed more control than he did, but he still couldn't stop this constant ache for her. She'd gotten into his head, and into his soul, in a very short time.

But he had to honor her request to be alone.

Unable to sleep, he walked outside. The late-night air hummed with a mixture of heat, humidity, and shrimp-like odors, the sound of the ocean mimicking the roaring of his heart.

He had to get a grip. He couldn't allow himself to obsess over Olivia to the point of forgetting the reason he'd been assigned to the case.

Yet even as he sacked out on the couch later, sleep eluded him. He still didn't know if Olivia's father had been involved in creating the virus. If so, how could he possibly tell Olivia? It would devastate her....

He finally drifted in and out of sleep, but was up by dawn, showered and dressed. By the time Olivia emerged from the bedroom, he had pancakes and bacon prepared.

She looked exhausted, but had managed to shower and had shed the sling. He wondered if she'd suffered any more nightmares.

He handed her a cup of coffee. "Did you sleep?"

"Not much," she admitted. "I have to make arrangements for my father's funeral today."

"I'll drop you off and let you take care of things while I meet with Detective Black." He fixed her a plate and gestured for her to sit and eat, although she had a truffle in her hands and was nibbling on it. "That is, unless you want me to stay with you."

Her gaze met his, the memory of the kiss lingering between them. "No…why don't you take me to pick up my car. I need to stop by the hospital to have these stitches removed before I go to the funeral home."

He narrowed his eyes. "I don't mind driving you."

"Listen, Craig, I appreciate you playing bodyguard, but you must have something more urgent to do on the case. I…don't want to hold you up."

Protecting her was just as important to him as the case, he realized again. A good reason he should back away.

"You were nearly killed three times, Olivia," he said, instead. "It's not safe for you to be alone."

She stiffened, sipped her coffee, then ate a couple of bites and pushed away the plate. "Then let's get started."

He cleared the dishes while she retrieved her purse. But as they neared the door, she suddenly stopped and held back, a stricken look coloring her eyes.

"What's wrong, Olivia?"

Her mouth tightened, her hand trembling as she lifted it to her cheek. "I…I don't know…but you're right. It's not safe out there."

He froze, one hand on the doorknob. That comment didn't sound like the independent, fearless Olivia at all.

"No, it's not," he murmured, "but we can't sit around and wait on this killer to strike again."

Her fingers clenched her purse strap. "I…have a bad feeling. Someone's been watching me. Watching the house."

His gaze cut to the French doors. "Did you see someone outside?"

She shook her head. "But I know they're out there. He's waiting to kill me. He wants us both dead."

He cupped her elbow in his hand and slowly coaxed her to the door, surprised at the fear in her eyes as he unfastened the latch. "All the more reason for us to leave, Olivia. I'll check and see if someone's following us while I drive."

She shrank against him as they walked to the car. Worry knotted his stomach at her odd reaction. Why was Olivia suddenly behaving as if she was afraid when she normally charged forward, meeting every challenge and obstacle with fearless determination?

"THE WOUND IS HEALING nicely," Dr. Elgin said as he removed the last stitch from Olivia's shoulder. "How are you feeling?"

Olivia rotated her arm. "Better. Thank you."

"No problem. Is there anything else I can do for you?"

"No, thanks." She checked her watch, grateful she'd finished her checkup early, then hurried from the office and phoned Dr. Carrington, the infectious disease specialist from the CDC who'd been flown in to consult on the virus investigation. Craig was supposed to be meeting with him and Hal Oberman, the director of the DPS, and checking into Shubert's medical reports while

Olivia had her stitches removed, but she needed to speak with the doctor in private.

"Dr. Carrington speaking."

"This is Olivia Thornbird. Please don't say anything, just listen."

"What is this about?" the doctor asked in a shrill tone.

"I'm working with Agent Horn, and don't want to alarm him, but I...think I might have contracted the virus you're studying. I'm in the hospital and want you to run some tests, but please don't say anything to anyone, especially Agent Horn."

"I see." Dr. Carrington hesitated. "I'll meet you in five minutes."

Olivia's insides quivered as she hung up and rode the elevator to the lab. Footsteps clicked behind her. She checked over her shoulder and thought a man in a dark suit was following her, so she ducked into a storage closet, then peeked through the cracks.

The voices began again, whispering warnings in her head, filling her mind with images of pain and death, with images of more suffering to come. But everything seemed so real, as if it were happening before her eyes.

Someone had sprayed a deadly germ in the air. People were breaking out in a rash. Some were choking, clawing at themselves until blood trickled from the scratches. Others screamed as pain knifed through their chests. Convulsions came next.

They begged for something, anything to ease the pain. The only answer was to die.

A small government faction had started the rash. Had planned to use it as a counterterrorist measure, but something had gone wrong....

A nurse passed out suicide pills, and the victims choked them down. Their bodies jerked, faces contorted, skin turned a pasty white. Then they dropped like flies.

Shadows pulled at her, tried to draw her into the darkness. The scent of death enveloped her. The metallic taste of blood filled her mouth.

The pill—it would be so easy. Take away the fear. The pain to come. The sight of all those suffering.

No, she had to fight the urge to take her life.

Hardly able to breathe, she clawed her way out of the closet and stumbled forward, but spots danced before her eyes. She was going to pass out. Drown in the endless well of darkness.

Just like the others.

Unless Dr. Carrington could help her.

DR. CARRINGTON SNAPPED his briefcase shut in a dismissive gesture. "Gentlemen, I have to go."

Craig narrowed his eyes at the change in Dr. Carrington's demeanor. He suddenly seemed agitated. In a hurry.

"But we're not finished," Oberman said in a harsh tone. "I want to know more about the virus."

Dr. Carrington hesitated, as if weighing something in his mind, then pinched the bridge of his nose. "I…I'm not sure if I should tell you this."

"What is it?" Craig asked.

He fiddled with his stethoscope, tapped the desk, looked everywhere but at them. "Patient-doctor confidentiality—"

"If this is about the virus," Craig barked, "you have to tell us. It could be a matter of national security."

Carrington frowned, then jammed his hands into his lab coat. "We may have a live victim."

Craig's heart raced. "What? Where?"

"She called in and wants to be tested."

"How do we know it's not a crank?" Oberman asked.

Dr. Carrington moved toward the door at a brisk pace, his Italian loafers clicking on the hard floor. "It could be, but I don't think so. The patient sounds truly worried."

Craig matched his pace. "Who is it?"

Carrington paused, gave him a long assessing look, then cleared his throat. "Dr. Thornbird's daughter, Olivia Thornbird."

Craig's stomach clenched. Dear God, Olivia couldn't be sick, could she?

And if she was, why the hell hadn't she told him?

Chapter Fourteen

Olivia's throat constricted at the sight of Craig trailing Dr. Carrington into the lab. She'd wanted to keep her suspicions to herself, but it was obvious from the grim expression in Craig's eyes that Dr. Carrington had already confided the reason for her call.

Craig didn't bother to speak, just shot her that close-mouthed, dark look, then stood silently while the doctor moved to her side.

"I thought patients and doctors shared confidentiality," Olivia said in an accusatory voice.

Dr. Carrington's eyes filled with apology. "I'm sorry, Miss Thornbird, but we're all here because of a potentially deadly virus that might be a public hazard. If there's a chance you have it, I had to alert the authorities."

Olivia glanced away, knowing he was right but hating the fact that Craig was present. The doctor she could handle. They were both impersonal, professionals, doing a job.

Not someone she cared about…

Of course, to her, Craig simply represented a job as well.

"Now, what makes you think you've contracted the virus?" Dr. Carrington asked in a concerned tone.

Olivia averted her gaze from Craig, but tension vibrated between them. "I…I haven't been feeling well."

"Headaches?"

"Yes."

"Ringing in the ears?"

"Yes."

Dr. Carrington ordered a nurse to bring supplies, then eased on rubber gloves and lifted Olivia's arm to check for a vein. "What else?"

"I've been feeling feverish, and…strange, as if someone was following me," Olivia continued. "Experiencing feelings of paranoia as if someone wants to kill me."

"Someone *has* been trying to kill you," Craig argued, as if denying that she might be ill.

Olivia glanced up, wondering if she misread the turmoil in his eyes and voice. "It's more than that," she said in a strained whisper. "I've been hearing voices, having hallucinations."

Dr. Carrington's brow knitted. "When did you first notice the symptoms?"

"Yesterday. But they're occurring more often," Olivia said. "It just came on so suddenly, this feeling…"

Dr. Carrington drew several vials of blood, then labeled them, his mouth in a grim line. "We'll run some tests, find out exactly what's going on with you, Miss Thornbird."

Olivia nodded. "How long will it take?"

"Don't worry, I'll rush it." Dr. Carrington folded his arms. "If you do have the virus, catching it in the early stages may be just the break we need to determine its origin and find a cure."

In spite of Dr. Carrington's optimism, hope drained from Olivia. So far, the virus had been fatal. "No one else has survived."

Craig moved up beside her. "We don't know yet that you even have the virus, Olivia," he said in a low voice. "And even if you do, catching it now will enable the doctors to treat you."

"But there isn't a cure," Olivia said. "And even if I survive, we don't know what kind of long-term side effects I'll have. Just look at what happened to Dr. Shubert."

Craig placed his hands on top of her shoulders, and turned her to face him. "Olivia, look at me."

She bit down on her lip, but reluctantly obeyed.

"We have no reason to believe the current virus we're studying had anything to do with the one he contracted," Craig said in a low voice. "Don't panic, and don't give up hope."

Olivia looked into Craig's eyes, felt the heat from his hands, the stirring of desire in her body. More regrets surfaced. She'd sacrificed love for her career. She'd never have the chance to have a family. And as much as she wanted to make love with Craig, she couldn't risk giving him the virus by becoming intimate with him now.

EMOTIONS WAGED A BATTLE within Craig. He had tried to comfort Olivia, but the truth stared him in the face, cold, hard, unforgiving. So far, they had a few details about the virus, its source, the way it attacked the body and how it was contracted. And everyone who'd gotten it had committed suicide.

If Olivia had the virus, she might die.

He wouldn't let that happen. He'd stay with her around the clock. Hospitalize her if he had to. Restrain her until they found a cure.

"I'll call you as soon as I receive the results," Dr. Carrington said. "Thankfully, we have determined that the virus isn't passed through physical contact or we'd have to put you in isolation. But I would like to hospitalize you overnight for observation and to run more tests."

"Can I go home and get some things?" Olivia asked.

"Actually, let me run this preliminary test first. If it's positive, I'll call you and you can come back in to be admitted."

"Fine."

Olivia looked so pale, Craig took her elbow and helped her up. "Let's talk to the doctors at CIRP one more time."

She nodded. "I'd like to see Dr. Fulton's reaction when he learns I may have contracted the virus."

"So would I." His cell phone rang as he and Olivia headed to his car. "Agent Horn."

"It's Devlin. I just got word that Milaski is in the States. I'm catching a plane now. We have agents searching for him. We think he may have recently been in Savannah."

"You definitely think there's a connection?"

"Yes. We've uncovered information that leads us to believe Milaski is spearheading a terrorist cell, and that Thornbird might have created the virus and sold it to this black market terrorist group. My guess is the European scientists discovered Thornbird's plan and were killed to silence them. We're looking into the location of the terrorist cell now."

Craig grimaced. If Thornbird was responsible, then he'd destroyed a half-dozen lives already and that might just be the beginning. Worse, his own daughter might die now because of it.

"We also think Thornbird may have been working on an antidote. But we haven't cracked his files yet. The team is getting close, though."

"Good, we need it." He angled his head away from Olivia as they made their way outside, then relayed the latest turn of events.

"Damn. Do you know how she contracted it?" Devlin asked.

"No." Craig remembered the fire, the smell of gas. But he didn't have any symptoms and he'd inhaled the same gas. Besides, the virus wasn't supposed to be airborne. So how was it possible that Olivia had become infected?

You're jumping the gun. You don't know for sure that she has.

Yet Olivia's worried expression and odd behavior indicated she might be ill. She wasn't normally a paranoid or weak person.

Dread hummed in the air as he hung up and they drove to CIRP, the gears grinding, breaking the quiet.

"I'm trying to understand how you could have become infected," Craig said, evading the issue that weighed heavily on his mind, the issue that had to be tormenting Olivia—was she going to die?

"Do you think that man injected me with it when I was in the hospital?" Olivia asked.

Craig shrugged. "It's possible. But it should have shown up in the blood work Dr. Elgin did before you left the hospital."

What other possibilities were there? If she hadn't been injected and the virus wasn't airborne, could she possibly have ingested it? He mentally ticked back over the last two days. Olivia had eaten all her meals with him. She'd barely been out of his sight.

Except at the hospital. "Olivia, did you eat anything at the hospital?"

She shook her head. "No. I couldn't stomach the food. The only thing I had was bottled water."

He mentally replayed their actions. When they'd arrived at his cabin, he'd made dinner. Then her co-worker had arrived with flowers and candy.

He swerved sideways and nearly hit the curb.

The truffles. Olivia liked chocolate—anyone could have discovered that detail.

He needed to have the candy tested. If they pinpointed the original source of the virus, maybe they could find the cure. And maybe someone at CIRP could create an antidote before it was too late.

His heart racing, he dialed Detective Black and asked him to pick up Jerry Renard for questioning. If Renard had given Olivia tainted chocolates, then he was guilty of attempted murder.

CRAIG SUDDENLY SWUNG the car around and headed in the opposite direction. The abrupt change and movement made Olivia dizzy, and she gripped the door handle, paranoia setting in again.

"What's wrong? Why did you ask Agent Devlin to pick up Jerry?"

"I have a hunch. We're going back to my cabin and grab those chocolates. I want to have them tested."

"You think I might have gotten the virus through the truffles?"

"If you weren't injected with the germ, it's possible you ingested it through food. Since the symptoms showed up within the last forty-eight hours, we'll look at that time period. I prepared your meals since you left the hospital."

"We ate at that diner once."

"But you and I had the same thing, and I'm not experiencing any symptoms." Craig tapped the steering wheel. "The only other thing you've had were those damn truffles."

"But Jerry gave those to me."

His lethal look sent a surge of horror through her.

"I can't believe Jerry would do such a thing. We've competed for bylines at the paper, but…he wouldn't try to kill me."

"Maybe he was desperate and decided to create a story so he could break it."

She twisted her hands in her lap, sweat beading on her palms. "Where would he get the virus?"

"I don't know. But he's an investigative reporter, I'm sure he has contacts. And he was in Iraq and Afghanistan before coming to Savannah." He paused and, when she didn't argue, continued, "Devlin said he thinks the leader of a terrorist cell, a man named Milaski, is here in Savannah. He believes that someone sold the virus to him. Maybe even to others."

Olivia's mind raced. "Oh, my God. Jerry has been investigating the possibility of a local terrorist group."

Tires squealed as he veered into the driveway. Remembering her father's diskette, Olivia hurried into the bedroom and retrieved it while Craig grabbed the box of chocolates. The next half hour passed in a blur as he dropped the truffles off at the hospital for testing.

While he met with the doctor, she excused herself to go to the restroom. Footsteps sounded in the hallway, and she peered outside, then hurried into a vacant office and inserted the disk in the computer, hoping their systems held a program to break the encryption. Again, she tried several passwords she thought her father might have used, but failed each time. In a last frantic attempt, she plugged in the date of her mother's death. Bingo. Information spilled onto the screen, part gibberish, but occasionally she made out a phrase or word, enough to realize the disk did have information about her mother's death.

The skin on the back of her neck prickled, and she suddenly spun around to see if someone was behind her. But the room was empty. Still, she felt eyes watching her, felt as if someone was breathing down her neck. Her hands trembling, she removed the disk and jammed it back in her purse. Why had her father saved this disk? Why hadn't he given it to someone? And what the hell was on it?

She remembered how he'd refused to pursue an investigation over her mother's death, and a sense of unease mushroomed inside her. What if he hadn't pursued it because he knew the truth and wanted to cover it up himself?

No. Her father wouldn't do such a thing. The paranoia was putting suspicions in her head that had to be groundless.

But what if he had known more about the virus than he'd admitted? What if he'd even had something to do with it falling into the hands of terrorists?

She swallowed hard. If she discovered he had, what would she do?

Could she bury the truth?

Craig's attitude toward journalism raced through her mind, making her wonder.

Then the ringing echoed in her ears again, and a sharp pain split her temple. She pressed her hand to her mouth to stifle a groan. But inside, her head reeled.

First, Craig had made her question Jerry's loyalties. Now she was questioning her father's.

This couldn't be happening.

She debated whether to give Dr. Carrington or Craig the disk as she hurried back to the doctor's office. After all, what if it had something on it that could help save lives, even her own? Then she had to turn it over…

Craig met her at the door. "Are you all right?"

She nodded. "Are you ready to go?"

"Yes." They walked back to the car in silence.

Craig slid his hand over hers as they climbed inside. "It's going to be okay, Olivia. Trust me."

She squeezed his hand and leaned against the seat, grateful for his support. So far, Craig had been nothing but honorable. He'd lived up to his promise to keep her informed and give her the story. The questions pertaining to the diskette plagued her. If it contained information that might help them with this virus, that might save lives, she couldn't hide it, or she'd lose her integrity.

She removed it and held it out to him. "Craig, I…found this at my father's."

His gaze cut toward her, eyes narrowed. "What's on it?"

"I don't know. I tried to look at it, but it's encrypted. Maybe you can find out."

"You were keeping something else from me?" His eyes darkened. "I thought we were working together."

"It's not like that," Olivia argued. "It was an old disk, stuffed in the attic. I had no idea if it related to something recent or not."

His mouth softened a fraction. "But you think it contains information about the virus?"

She shrugged. "I don't know. No telling how long it's been up in the attic. It might be data about an older research project, but I saw my mother's name on it, so who knows."

"Your father must have hidden it for a reason."

She nodded, endless possibilities in her mind. Some she understood. Others…she didn't want to consider.

"I'll have it checked out." Craig brushed her cheek with the pad of his thumb, lowering his voice. "Maybe it's what we've been looking for."

Something to save her life. He didn't have to say the words, but the silent acknowledgement lingered between them anyway. Odd how she'd thought of Craig as the Iceman, cold and unfeeling, yet he was soothing her now, offering her hope in a near hopeless situation. But he was making promises he might not be able to keep.

She still had to beat a deadly virus, one that no one else had ever survived.

And if she discovered her father had had something to do with the virus, what would she do? Could she ask Craig to bury the truth?

DR. FULTON PULLED AT the frayed collar of his white shirt. "You think you've contracted the virus, Miss Thornbird?"

"Yes."

"We think she may have ingested the germ through tainted chocolates," Craig said. "Dr. Carrington is testing them now."

"What have you learned from my father's research?"

Fulton paced the small confines of his cluttered office. "So far, not much more than what we discussed the first time we talked."

Craig cleared his throat, sensing Fulton wasn't being quite honest. "Was there anything in Thornbird's notes to indicate an antidote for the virus?"

"No. If there's a cure, Thornbird hadn't discovered it," Fulton said. "I need to speak to Dr. Carrington when he gets your blood work back, Miss Thornbird. In fact, if you'll allow me to draw some blood samples, there are a few tests I'd like to run."

"Sure," Olivia said. "I'll do anything I can to expedite the research and find a cure."

"Have you ever heard of a man named Iska Milaski?" Craig asked as Fulton drew blood.

Fulton shook his head, his bushy eyebrows wagging as he frowned. "No, who is he?"

"The head of a terrorist cell. We believe he's in Savannah," Craig said, grateful that their informant, Harlam, had come through for them. "We believe Milaski either has access to or is after the virus germ."

Fulton's head jerked up. "My God, you think that the virus is terrorist-related?"

"It looks that way now," Craig said. "Do any of the scientists here have issues with the government?"

"You mean would one of our doctors sell this germ to a terrorist group?" Fulton stored and labeled the vials of blood, then pressed a bandage over Olivia's arm before looking back at Craig. "That's ridiculous. Besides, I thought the virus originated in Europe. Shouldn't you be looking at some of the research facilities there for answers?"

"We have agents checking that angle," Craig said, wondering again about Thornbird. If he'd thought the government had covered up his wife's murder, maybe this new virus was his revenge. "You still didn't answer my question, Dr. Fulton. Is there anyone on staff who might have a grudge against the government or the U.S.? Someone who'd use the virus to make a statement or to frighten the public? Or maybe someone who thought they were selling to a militia group to use against terrorists?"

"No." Fulton gestured toward the door. "Now I need to get back to work. If Miss Thornbird is suffering from this virus, time is of the essence."

Craig nodded. So far, it was the only thing he and Fulton agreed on.

AFTER THEY LEFT CIRP, Craig drove Olivia to the Savannah Funeral Home to make arrangements for her father.

If Fulton created the virus, he could alter the data, cover it up.

Craig had obviously agreed and had dropped the disk at the hospital for the CDC doctor to review.

"What kind of service would you like?" the funeral director, Harvey Binger, a small overweight man with a double chin and toupee, asked.

Olivia struggled to tune out the voices in her head so she could focus. "I... Just something simple. I'm afraid my father didn't have many friends, but I'm sure some of his colleagues will come to show their respect."

"Do you want to use our chapel for the service?"

"Yes."

"Let me show you our selection of caskets. We have a variety of models, ranging in prices and design, everything from ornate and elegant to simple..."

His voice droned on as he escorted her to another area, a large room that was ice-cold, filled with shiny bronze and pewter-gray caskets. Elevator music piped over the speakers, adding a melancholy feel to the morose atmosphere. Olivia's stomach fluttered with nausea as she imagined her father lying on the layers of satin.

Then an image of her own body being placed inside another coffin and lowered into the ground replaced the image, and her knees buckled.

"Olivia?"

Craig caught her, his husky voice barely audible above the incessant yelling and ringing in her ears.

She pointed to a gray casket with off-white lining. "That one is fine." Desperate for air, she raced toward the door, then hurled herself outside into the muggy heat.

CRAIG RUSHED AFTER Olivia, his cell phone ringing. "Horn here."

"It's Detective Black. I have Renard at the station."

"Good, hold him. I'll be there in a few minutes."

He found Olivia leaning against the porch rail outside, inhaling the humid summer air, looking pale. She desperately needed rest. He wanted to take her home, tuck her into bed and hold her. But he had to interrogate Renard. And he didn't want to leave her alone, not when she was so vulnerable. Not when he knew the fate of the other victims.

He stroked her back, rubbing small circles near her spine. "You've been through a hell of a lot these last three days, Olivia. I'm amazed you're still standing."

Her gaze swung to his, the shadows of fear and truths inside. She might not be standing for very long. Or be alive much longer.

His heart swelled with compassion and admiration. Another layer of that self-protective armor was chiseled away. He reached to pull her into his arms, but his cell phone trilled again. "Agent Horn."

"This is Dr. Carrington. I have results from the blood tests we ran on Olivia Thornbird and from the truffles."

His heart skipped a painful beat. "And?"

"She's definitely been infected." Dr. Carrington's voice warbled slightly. "And the truffles were tainted with the germ."

OLIVIA WONDERED at Craig's sudden brooding as they drove to the police station. When he'd hung up from the phone call, his expression had gone completely rigid. He hadn't spoken since. Not even to explain the call. He'd simply driven like a madman to the precinct.

Jerry glared at them as they entered the police interrogation room. "What in the hell is going on?"

"I might ask you the same question," Craig snarled.

Betrayal sliced through Olivia as she imagined Jerry buying the truffles, actually injecting the germ into them, then hand-delivering them to her door. She didn't want to believe he was capable of such a thing.

Jerry leaned forward, thick hands on his knees. "I

don't have a clue as to what this is about. But I have work to do, so get on with it. These detectives have been acting like I've murdered someone."

The breath rushed from Olivia's chest. "I'm not dead yet."

Craig's jaw snapped tight, and Olivia gripped the side of the table, the world tilting sideways as realization dawned. The phone call…the tests were back, and they were positive. Craig hadn't said anything, but that was the reason he'd grown so sullen. He was stalling, not wanting to deliver the bad news.

"Olivia, please wait outside," Craig said in a rough voice.

"No." She straightened, summoning every ounce of courage she possessed. "You promised me a story, and I'm going to get it."

"Olivia, no—"

"You got the results from my tests, didn't you, Craig?"

His gaze latched on to hers, held for a long moment, a flicker of regret and sorrow betraying his calm. That slight reaction wrenched her heart, but confirmed what she already knew. The voices that had been whispering to her were real.

And soon she would be dead.

No, she would fight it.

But if death were her fate, she deserved to know the truth first.

She gestured toward Jerry, barely managing to stand as the ringing in her ears intensified. "I have a right to hear what he has to say."

Craig gave her another anguished look, but it faded

as he faced Jerry. "Mr. Renard, each of the suicide victims in Savannah has been diagnosed with a rare and unidentified virus that we now believe was part of a terrorist attack. You gave Olivia a box of truffles that contains the germ for that virus." He paused, his voice lowering to a lethal pitch. "You are not only under suspicion of four murders so far, but unless you tell us everything you know about the virus—"

"You may be looking at one more," Olivia finished. "And I don't intend to die without finding out the reason."

Chapter Fifteen

Craig studied Renard's body language. The shocked expression. The instant beading of sweat on his upper lip. The wild-eyed panic.

"I don't understand what you're talking about," Renard protested. "I don't know anything about a virus."

Which would be true *if* the man was innocent. So far, by some miracle, the police had kept it from leaking to the press and the public. But Craig wasn't convinced Renard was telling the truth.

"That virus has mysterious consequences. You hand-delivered the package that infected Olivia. I was there when you gave it to her, remember?" He clutched the shaking man by the collar. "And you had the audacity to act concerned about her while you gave it to her. Why did you infect her, Renard? To get the story? Or are you working for a terrorist group?"

"Whoa…" Renard held up a hand, the college ring on his third finger glimmering under the bold light. "I was investigating a terrorist group, but I'm certainly not a member of it."

"What group is it and where is the cell located?"

"I don't have enough yet to know for sure if they're planning anything—"

"The name and location." Craig released him abruptly, then shoved a pen and pad in front of Renard. Renard scribbled an address of a local warehouse.

"Your contact?"

"A hooker named Candy. She met this guy, Gustav Vironsky, and overheard a cell phone conversation between him and another man that sounded suspicious," Renard replied. "But she doesn't know the leader and isn't involved herself."

"Does the name Iska Milaski sound familiar?"

Renard hesitated, the pencil point breaking beneath his grip. "I've heard the name, but never met him."

Craig clenched his collar again. "Now, about the virus. Where did it come from?"

"I told you I don't know," Renard exclaimed.

Olivia paced in front of him. "For God's sake, Jerry, you tried to kill me and now you're denying it—"

"I didn't send the chocolates," Renard said, his shoulders slumping slightly. "When we received word at the paper that you were injured, the secretary ordered the balloons."

"And the candy?" Craig asked.

Renard scrubbed a hand over his reddening face. "The box was delivered earlier that day for Olivia. I...when I saw it, I grabbed it and pretended it was from me."

Olivia looked appalled. "Why would you do that?"

Renard ducked his head slightly. "I thought you were on to a big story. I was hoping that if I played nice to you, you might let me in on it."

Craig hissed in disgust. "You have no scruples when

getting a story, right, Renard? You'll even stoop to using your friends."

Renard shifted nervously. "The end justifies the means." He faced Olivia. "Don't look at me that way. You'd do the same thing, and you know it."

Olivia swallowed and shook her head. "I have morals, Jerry."

"But you still use people. That's why you're in bed with the feds now, isn't it?" Renard snarled. "For a story."

Craig glared at him, seeing the calculating man for what he was. It took every ounce of restraint he had not to punch him out.

But Renard's words rose to haunt Craig. *The end justifies the means.* Hadn't he always told himself the same thing? And he and Olivia had made a deal…but they hadn't slept together.

Not yet, anyway.

Olivia didn't bother to restrain herself, though. She slapped Renard's face, the sharp blow resounding through the room. Renard's stunned look was almost funny.

"Who delivered the chocolates?" Craig asked, his mouth twitching as Renard rubbed his red jaw.

"Some guy from a local delivery service," Renard grunted.

"Did the box come with a card?"

"No. It simply had Olivia's name on it."

Craig rammed a finger in Renard's chest. The perp had intentionally targeted Olivia. "Don't move. I'll be right back. And don't touch *her.*" He gave Olivia a long sideways look, then exited and met Detective Black in the adjoining room.

"I'll check out the delivery service," Black said. "And I've already checked this guy's record, Horn. He's been caught lying to the police before."

Fury sparked Craig's blood as he rushed back to the interrogation room. Olivia had taken a seat at the table opposite Renard, her skepticism and distrust of Renard obvious by her rigid posture and the distance she kept between them.

Good. Whether Renard was telling the truth or not, he didn't want her anywhere near the bastard.

OLIVIA DIDN'T BAT AN EYE when Craig ordered Jerry to be tossed into a holding cell for the night, although Jerry protested that he was innocent and they were violating his rights.

"Damn man will learn something about rights in the pen," Craig growled.

Olivia nodded, but Jerry's comments bothered her. She and Craig had cut a deal about the story. And they had come close to jumping into bed together.

But she hadn't wanted to make love to Craig for the story…

What about him? Was he simply using her?

She continued to silently ponder the case while Craig accompanied the team that had been dispatched to the address Jerry had given them. Detective Fox offered her a notepad, and she scribbled notes and ideas for the article she planned to write when the investigation ended…if she lived that long.

What would be her angle?

The families of the victims? The terrorist cell and its justification for taking innocent lives? The threat of chemical and germ warfare and the ramifications on the governments and people involved?

The personal fear of the public when they discovered information had been withheld from them? Or her personal fear as a victim herself?

The dark clouds of terror engulfed her, the chatter of the officers in the precinct and the hiss of perpetrators being brought in echoing around her as if she'd fallen into a dark abyss and would never escape. The odor of stale coffee and body sweat permeated the room, the sounds of vile language and snickers from a prisoner adding to the clamor of gloomy reality.

Craig and the other detectives strode into the precinct, their expressions grim.

She stood abruptly. "Did you find Milaski?"

Craig shook his head. "The warehouse was empty. Someone must have tipped them off."

The muscles at the back of her neck knotted. Time was closing in, yet they were no nearer finding the truth than they had been the day the first Savannah suicide victim had taken his life.

"I've phoned Devlin to update him," Craig said. "Maybe he has another lead. Then I'll take you home to rest."

She offered him a faint smile, although hope dwindled with every passing minute.

Craig and the detectives conferred while she gathered her notes. Too exhausted to argue, she went willingly with Craig when he insisted he drive her back to his cabin. The stirrings of fear mingled with images of death as she drifted to sleep inside the car. Then suddenly the car stopped, and she felt Craig's hands go around her shoulders. She struggled to wake up, but Craig lifted her and carried her inside his cabin.

The dim light of the lamp bathed the room in a soft glow as he placed her on the bed. Her head throbbed, and her ears were ringing with the incessant voices.

You'll be next, Olivia. You can already feel the illness threading through your veins. Plucking at your rational thoughts. Tossing shadows in front of your eyes. Making you see that life after death is a reprieve from the loneliness and pain.

Suddenly aching and afraid to be alone, she clutched at Craig's arm. "Please don't leave me."

Craig lowered himself beside her and cradled her against him. "I won't go, Olivia. Don't worry, go to sleep."

She cuddled into the covers, savoring the warmth of his muscular arms around her, and did as he said. Curling up against his strong hard body felt like a forbidden pleasure, but for once in her life, she allowed herself the privilege of physical comfort.

In her dreams, the demons tore her from his arms and threw her into a fiery pit. Her father waited, burning among the ashes, his pain-filled pleas piercing the night. Her mother hovered somewhere beyond, looking angelic, but just as she reached for Olivia to save her, Olivia fell into the scorching flames.

CRAIG CRADLED Olivia to him, his heart racing as he contemplated the fact that she might die.

It wasn't possible. He couldn't let it happen.

He'd failed his sister and Olivia's father. But he couldn't fail Olivia. She didn't deserve this fate.

She cried out, trembling against him, and tendrils of fear and admiration, along with primal protective instincts, were roused within him. He hadn't meant to fall for her. Had vowed he wouldn't.

But he'd never met anyone like Olivia. Gutsy. Strong. Persistent. Sexy as hell.

And his time with her might be short-lived.

He smoothed the hair from her cheek and caressed her soft skin, drinking in the sweet smell of her shampoo and body fragrance. Olivia was a bright light in the dark world that had become his life. He'd seen the depravities of mankind, watched the weak fall. Seen innocents killed in the name of revenge. Seen the consequences of this virus.

He'd always thought getting involved would endanger the woman he was with, that she wouldn't be strong enough to stand up to the challenge.

But not Olivia.

Except this time, the challenge might beat her. Might beat them both.

The clock was ticking. The virus attacked quickly. They might only have days… And the virus wasn't transmitted through human contact, not like AIDS.

She opened her eyes, the fear dissipating slightly as their gazes connected.

"Craig?"

Her voice sounded like a featherlight whisper. "Yeah?"

She gently pressed one hand on his cheek, her lips parted, then she kissed him. Her lips felt like rose petals, the silky softness gliding against his mouth in a slow sensual torture that triggered his own need. "Thanks for staying with me."

"God, Olivia…" He lowered his head against hers, felt her breath bathe his neck, the hunger in her sigh as she brushed another kiss across the underside of his chin. He was drowning in desire.

"I don't want to lose you," he ground out.

She made a soft sound of denial, then yearning rose in the depth of her eyes. "Let's forget the investigation tonight," she whispered.

How could he not think about it?

"Just make me feel alive, Craig."

"I'm not going to let you die," he promised. A groan erupted from within him as he cupped her face in his hands and forced her to look at him. "Don't even think like that, do you hear me?"

"Please, Craig. I just want you…to make me feel tonight."

The dam of control he normally kept erected split and burst open. He had to have her. "I want you, too, Olivia." He traced a finger over her lips, feeling them swell beneath his touch. "Don't think of this as the last time, but as the first."

With that husky promise, he claimed her mouth in a sensual foray that sent desire rippling through his loins. He instantly hardened, desperate hunger nearly choking him. But he had to give Olivia pleasure. Had to make her feel loved, that he wanted her more than he had ever wanted another woman. "Do you have any idea how beautiful you are?" he whispered.

Olivia sighed and pressed her fingers deep into his back, pulling him harder against her. "I need you inside me, Craig."

Her soft admission nearly put him over the edge, but

he'd waited too long to rush, so he whispered sultry words, promises of what he would do to her as he slowly peeled away her blouse. Then he dropped tender kisses along her jaw and neck, and slowly, almost reverently, kissed the outside of her scar. She blushed and tried to cover herself, but he shook his head. "You're absolutely beautiful. Perfect." He nuzzled her neck, his voice a husky whisper. "But tell me if I hurt you."

"You won't." Desire softened her eyes as she smiled at him. Then he tasted the sensitive skin of her ear, teasing her until she buckled beneath him. "I need you, Craig."

He dove back to take her mouth in a virtual frenzy of passionate kisses, each one deeper and longer, each one driving home the fact that he wanted to be inside her, that he soon would be.

She moaned and clawed her fingers through his hair, dragging him closer, sliding her leg in between his to tease him. The satiny strands of hair tickled his nose, invited his hands to play in the tresses and he did. Her breasts swelled into his chest, the turgid peaks begging for his touch. Unable to withstand the torture any longer, he lowered his head, skimmed kisses along the top of her bra, pried the lace away with his teeth, then sank into heaven by closing his mouth around a tight nipple. He licked and suckled it, plucking her other nipple with his finger as he wedged his leg between her thighs. She spread her legs for him, writhed into his hardness, tore at his clothes until he rose and stripped off the layers that separated them, leaving only skin and heart and soul between them.

The sight of her naked before him was incredible—

her eyes glowing with wanton desires, her breathing labored as she offered herself to him, and he loved her all over, kissing and licking down to her belly, the firm calf that led upward to the secrets he wanted to explore. But he moved slowly, tasting every inch, planting long tender kisses along her inner thighs until she cried out.

"Craig, please, I need you."

"I need you, too." He dipped his head and pressed his tongue to her center, teasing and inciting her with each stroke until she shuddered, and he felt the sweet bliss of her release.

She reached for him, begged him closer, and he slid on a condom, then moved over her, allowing only a brief hesitation for her to adjust to his size before he thrust inside her. The pleasure was so intense, the pain of waiting excruciating, but the reward more earth-shattering and titillating than he'd ever imagined.

Tonight might have to last them both forever.

No, he stifled the thought, sank himself into her again, then withdrew his erection and teased her honeyed folds, stroking slowly and sliding into her as he cupped and lifted her hips to fill her more completely. She clawed at his back, then wrapped her legs around him, biting at his neck as his lips skated over her mouth. Erotic sensations ebbed and flowed, burned within him, reached a crescendo as she came apart in his arms again. Groaning in pleasure, he finally allowed himself to climax. She cried out again as her body tightened and convulsed around him, then sensations spiraled through him as they rode the wave of ecstasy together.

Olivia had never felt so loved in her entire life. She

wrapped herself around Craig, shutting out her fears temporarily as the aftermath of their lovemaking settled over her. A thousand blissful, tingling sensations traveled along her nerve endings, pure erotic pleasure seeping through her.

"That was wonderful, Craig."

He gently feathered her hair from her cheek and kissed her again. "Yeah, and remember what I said," he whispered. "That was only the beginning."

Sadness threatened to steal her joy, but she banished it. If she only had a short time to live, she wanted every second to count. She was in love with Craig. She supposed she had been for some time.

But she couldn't declare her love now, not when she might be dying.

The evil voices whispered again from the far recesses of her mind, warring for space in her head, but she shut them out.

As if he read her thoughts, he swept her into his arms and kissed her again, this time slowly, methodically, as if his touch could erase any pain or any lingering doubt that they were meant to be together.

She pushed him to his back, determined to show him that she wasn't giving in to the illness yet, that she was the same strong woman he had first met.

"Is your shoulder all right?" he murmured.

"Everything's perfect." She trailed her finger over his chest, playing with the thick tufts of dark hair, following the trail down to where his arousal pulsed between her legs. One touch sent her body into a frenzy of heated desire, shuddering and begging for more.

He groaned, a primal hunger darkening his eyes as

he cupped her breasts in his palms. She swayed and let him suckle her, then dipped her head and kissed a path down his belly until her lips closed over his swollen sex.

His groan of approval ignited heat within her belly, the thick hardness of him filling her mouth as heady as when he'd been inside her. Finally, when he could take it no more, she impaled herself on him, her body clenching with erotic sensations as she rode him, her release even more intense this time at the sight of the pleasure in his eyes.

They made love again and again through the night, the final time in the early morning hours just before dawn peeked through the sky. And as the first rays of sunlight filtered through the shades, she curled up next to him and fell asleep. Nestled safely in his arms, lying sated by his side, she dreamed of tomorrow.

But in her sleep, the voices returned, taunting her that tomorrow might never come....

CRAIG'S CELL PHONE RANG an hour later. Not wanting to wake Olivia, he grabbed it, strode into the den and closed the bedroom door. "Special Agent Horn."

"Detective Black. The fire at CIRP was definitely not accidental. There was evidence that someone tampered with the wiring."

"I figured as much."

"We think we've located a vacant warehouse where Milaski is holed up," Black continued. "I've got a team ready to go."

"I'll meet you there. What's the location?"

"River Street." Black recited the address.

"Get a car over to watch the house. Olivia's asleep.

I don't want her tagging along on this. It might get too dangerous."

"I'll send one right over."

Craig hung up, tiptoed into the bedroom, grabbed a pair of slacks and a shirt and rushed into the bathroom. Assuming Olivia would sleep for hours, he kissed her on the cheek, scribbled her a note, then grabbed his gun and hurried out the door. A uniformed officer pulled up in a patrol car, Craig waved, then hopped into his car and sped toward River Street. Finding Milaski might just be the break they needed to solve this case.

And to save Olivia's life.

She stood on a grassy hill overlooking the Savannah River, a long white dress swirled around her ankles, the scent of roses wafting around her as a guitar strummed the Wedding March. Sunlight glimmered off the rows of white chairs and the gazebo where she would be married. The minister waited, Bible open in his hand, while Craig, dressed in a black tux, turned to face her. He was holding out his hand....

A dark cloud rolled across the sky, obliterating the sun. Shadows rose like dragons breathing fire. Sinister voices reverberated through the fog. "They're going to get you. You're going to die." The shrill ringing grew louder, more incessant as pain sliced through her temple.

She covered her ears with her hands and cried out, then jerked awake, trembling and drenched in sweat. It took a second for her to orient herself. She was in Craig's bed. Sunlight streamed through the windows.

But Craig was gone. And the telephone was ringing.

Wondering where Craig was and if the call might be important, she dragged on her shirt and padded to the den. The phone trilled again, then the answering machine clicked on.

"Craig, this is your father. Why the hell aren't you answering your mobile?" Senator Horn snapped. "We have to have a conference call with the head of the DPS today. Oberman wants to know what you're doing to keep that Thornbird woman quiet. We both agree that you might be right, that Dr. Thornbird might be a traitor. I hope to God that you've found the source of the virus by now and can make this thing go away before the people ever have to find out. Call my cell as soon as you get this message."

Olivia gasped and stumbled against the sofa as the phone clicked into silence. What did Craig's father mean—*what was Craig doing to keep her quiet?* And when had Craig decided her father was a traitor?

She glanced down at her near naked body, remembering their heated lovemaking, and a sense of betrayal knifed through her.

No. Craig wouldn't have slept with her just to sway her to keep quiet or keep her from writing the article, would he?

As a POLICE CAR PARKED in front of Craig Horn's cabin, he gripped the can of gasoline from the floor of the truck, his temper surfacing in spite of his razor-sharp control. An image of the beautiful fire lighting up the predawn sky, the flames licking and sucking the life from Olivia Thornbird and that federal agent, would have been such a satisfying sight. He could see the pictures in the paper. Photographs of ash and debris. Of their bodies charred beyond recognition. Black soot falling like rain.

The headlines glorifying him for getting away.

They'd never know his name. His face. His identity. Because he could change it all in a second.

And now Horn had left and she was all alone.

A smile tipped his mouth. Hell, maybe this would be more fun. He could watch the torture on Horn's face when he discovered the fire that had destroyed his house.

And the woman who'd been sleeping in his bed, how her creamy lithe body had been turned into brittle black ashes.

Agents weren't supposed to get involved with reporters or suspects or informants. But Horn had no restraint.

Not as he did. Because he had been taught by the master.

Nothing could deter him from his job. His chosen profession. Or the publicity he would get when it was all finished.

So far, Miss Thornbird had been a disappointment. His boss had banked on the fact that she would go public with her father's suicide. That she'd spread the word about the virus and create mass hysteria. He wanted that as well.

He would have reveled in watching the people wonder where and when the next strike would come and who the next victim would be.

But the woman had failed to do her part. Now she was completely expendable.

He turned his attention back to the more immediate

problem, the chunky cop eating a bear claw at the wheel of the police car.

Adrenaline surged through him as he spat onto the ground, the gloves on his hands crinkling in the heat. Hmph. The cop. A minor complication. He set the gasoline can on the floor of his truck, climbed out and stalked toward the police car.

The stupid lard-ass would never suspect a thing.

Just another life for the cause.

One more, then Olivia Thornbird…

Chapter Sixteen

Had Craig been using her all along?

He never loved you, Olivia. And his work is more important to him than you or else he wouldn't have left you alone, knowing you might be dying.

He'd probably thought by cozying up to her she'd confide something about her father, something that would incriminate him.

More paranoid than ever, she reread the note Craig had left her. He thought they'd found Milaski. Yet, even though he'd agreed to share information with her, to give her the story, he'd left her behind with the scent of their lovemaking still lingering on her skin.

She spotted Craig's briefcase, snapped it open and shuffled through the papers inside. A folder on her father drew her eye, and then another—a file marked with her name.

She sank back on the sofa, horrified as she skimmed the contents—the file included background information on her and her dad, as well as speculation about her father's possible involvement in creating the virus.

Craig actually thought her father had sold it to the terrorist faction. That this virus might be a mutant strain developed from the one that had killed her mother.

Which meant he also suspected that her father was involved in her mother's death. But he hadn't shared that theory, either. Not even when she'd given him the disk.

Instead of being honest, he'd urged her to trust him, had seduced her until she was mindless to do anything but be putty in his hands.

Shock, pain, hurt slammed into her, knocking the wind from her lungs.

Sure, she might have had a few fleeting moments where she'd doubted her father, but she'd dismissed the doubts quickly.

She swallowed hard, then glanced at the file on her. Information on her friends was listed. Past lovers, too, though there had been very few. And there was the incident where she'd been arrested for underage drinking and vandalism. Then there were photos of her in various protest marches. Pro animal rights, save the environment...

What had Craig been looking for? Something to incriminate her? An angle so he could blackmail her into cooperating in case she decided to print the story without his consent? Or had he thought *she'd* known about the virus?

A sense of betrayal shot through her again. She had trusted him more than any man she'd known. Had given him her body and her heart. Had promised to hold off on the story until he approved it.

But he didn't intend to release news about the virus at all. He'd planned to make love to her, then use her feelings to convince her to bury the story.

But what about the citizens' rights? She'd made a

vow to herself years ago, to her mother and then her father when he died, that she'd protect the people from cover-ups. And if she didn't, more people would die.

Again the images surfaced—the people dying by the dozens. The suicide pills being dispensed...

She didn't have a choice anymore. If Craig wasn't going to tell them the truth, then she had to. Besides, maybe by airing it, they'd get a lead and stop this killer before he struck again.

She rubbed her arms, a clammy feeling overwhelming her. The room was closing around her again, trapping her. A rash was spreading on her lower arms. Her breath rasped out as she pulled the top of her shirt apart. Small red splotches dotted her upper chest.

The symptoms of the virus were growing more prominent. She was getting sicker by the minute.

A sob built in her throat as she ran to the bedroom, threw on some clothes and headed to the door. She'd ask the policeman to drive her to the newspaper, then tell her story. No, she'd go to the TV station. Warn the public. They couldn't let this virus spread any further.

She made it to the door, but a wave of panic seized her. Sweat broke out on her face and body, and she trembled, the room spinning. She grabbed the door to steady herself and clung to it, willing herself to go outside. But outside someone waited to finish her off. She could feel him hiding in the shadows. His breath on the fine hairs at her nape.

Her fingers shook, her chest constricting. She couldn't make herself open the door.

Now she understood how trapped her father had felt, how the paralyzing fear had consumed him.

She slithered to the floor in a pool of nervous sweat, bowed her head and covered herself with her arms. She knew the paranoia was affecting her judgment. And she didn't want to give in to the illness.

But she didn't want to drag it out, either, or die alone.

CRAIG JOINED Detective Black and Fox, along with the SWAT team Black had commandeered, outside the empty warehouse on River Street. The place was nearly deserted, the building on the verge of dilapidation, the stench of wine and urine strong in the air.

"You're sure he's in there?" Craig asked as he scanned the cobblestoned street and riverbank nearby.

"An informant phoned, said a big deal was supposed to go down today between two foreigners. This was the address he gave us."

"Could be drugs or guns," Craig suggested.

"He heard Milaski's name in conjunction with the deal," Detective Fox said. "Word on the streets is that even the people who know him are terrified of him and what he might do. And there's word of a hired killer, too, someone trained by a man they called the master. No name for him though."

Black motioned for the team to prepare for attack, then Craig led the way as they surrounded the building. He ducked low and half crawled to the side, peering in through the dirt-coated window. "I see three men, no four. The big, tall one in back, that's Milaski?"

"Yes."

"There's a black duffel bag on the floor."

"Let's move." Black gave the count and Craig plunged through the window. Three SWAT officers stormed the door, a small team remained outside to circle the building, and Black and Fox covered the back.

"This is the FBI, the building is surrounded," Craig shouted. "Put your hands up and drop your weapons."

But no one surrendered. Gunfire broke out, the bullets flying. Craig dove behind a stack of crates, barely avoiding a hit in the chest while two SWAT team members burst through.

Seconds later, it was all over. Three men lay dead, their bloody bodies strewn across the concrete like wounded enemy soldiers. Craig and the detectives picked their way across the shattered glass and bodies. Then an engine roared outside, and Craig raced to the back door.

"Milaski's getting away!" Craig shouted. "Black sedan. I can't get a license plate."

Detective Black called in an APB, while Detective Fox raced to the side to get the police car.

Black searched the duffel bag. "It's empty. If he had the virus, he took it with him."

"I'll stay here till CSI arrives," Black said. "Go ahead with Fox."

Craig ran to join Fox in the car chase. They tore through the streets of Savannah, racing to keep up with the black sedan. The siren wailed, and Fox honked at tourists crowding the street, jaywalking and blocking their way. The sedan spun through an alley; the driver gunned it and whipped onto a side street. Fox hit the gas, veered around a garbage truck and nearly smashed into an oncoming car.

Tires squealed and the car slid, but Fox righted it and barreled on, yelling at the driver who hadn't given him the right of way. They combed the streets, circling around the squares, then headed toward the interstate, but they lost their suspect in the traffic.

Unwilling to give up, they cruised up and down the Savannah streets again, scanning the intersections and turnoffs. A group of kids from a summer camp crossed the road and a group of sailors followed, slowing traffic.

"There he is!" Craig shouted.

Fox punched the brakes, backed up and swung through the intersection, but couldn't turn because there was a one-way street. He had to go down another block and circle back.

"He's headed toward the drawbridge."

Craig gripped the dash. "We have to catch him."

Fox sped through a caution light, turned the corner and raced toward the drawbridge, but just as he drove onto the bridge, the siren boomed through the air, and the crossbars swung down, cutting him off. The sedan flew across the bridge and disappeared down the road leading to Catcall Island. "I'll call Black, tell him to get a chopper to search the area."

Craig nodded, but failure twisted at his gut. All this, and they'd come away without Milaski or the virus.

When he returned to Olivia, he'd hoped to tell her that they'd cracked the case, that they had the virus and an antidote.

But now he had nothing to offer, not even hope.

OLIVIA ROCKED HERSELF back and forth, fighting the shadows and voices, struggling not to let the paranoia rule her. She was stronger than it. She could survive. She would not let the virus take her life. She would hold on, and they would find a cure.

But the others had to know so they could save themselves. It was her job to inform them…Craig would have to understand.

Craig—where was he now?

She was so confused. Her mind was losing bits and pieces of conversations, of reality. She couldn't remember where he'd gone. Had he even told her?

Dragging her hands down from her head, she inhaled several calming breaths, then forced herself to crawl to the door. One inch. Two. She could make it.

Perspiration trickled down her neck and arms, and her hands trembled as she grabbed her purse, then turned the knob.

Panic clogged her throat, and she fell back against the wall, fear immobilizing her. Even as a little girl, Olivia had not been afraid of anything. Not the bullies in school. Not the athletes who laughed when she'd failed to make the basketball team. Not the dark, when her mother and father had left her alone to go to work.

She couldn't let fear possess her now.

Inhaling again, she clutched the doorknob, bit down on her lip and surged to her feet, then threw herself out into the sunlight. The bright rays nearly blinded her, but she ordered herself to move her legs, her feet, one step at a time.

Suddenly a hand gripped her elbow. "Miss Thornbird, are you all right?"

She made a pitiful sound, then nodded. "I need a ride to the television station."

"Are you sure? You look ill."

"Yes, I'm sure." She suddenly pulled back and stared at him. His voice sounded oddly familiar. Made a chill run up her spine. "Who are you?"

"Officer Batterson, ma'am. Agent Horn phoned me to watch the house while he took care of business."

She squinted to discern his features, but the image of the man who'd attacked her in the hospital bled through the hazy fog enveloping her, one man's face shifting sideways to replace the other. This man had a beard, though; he wasn't the attacker. And he was holding up his badge.

"All right. Then you can drive me."

"Yes, ma'am." He ushered her toward the squad car, and she climbed inside, grateful to escape the heat and bright lights as he shifted gears and veered onto the street.

She was safe now. Officer Batterson would protect her. He would drive her to the television station and she would tell her story.

The scenery passed in a blur as he drove. Olivia twined her hands together, trying to focus on what she would say on camera. The police car pulled up to the TV station, and Officer Batterson helped her out, then escorted her inside.

A receptionist greeted them. "What can I do for you?"

"I'm Olivia Thornbird, *Savannah Sentinel*. I need to speak to one of your news correspondents immediately."

The woman tugged at the collar of her silk blouse, looking nervous. "Wasn't your father that doctor who killed himself a few days ago?"

"Yes, and I have important news about the Savannah Suicides."

The woman jumped up and jogged toward a back office. Seconds later, Paul Fleshman, a slim blond man in his mid-thirties and one of the lead news reporters for the station, appeared. "What can I do for you, Miss Thornbird?"

She swayed slightly as she stepped forward. "You can put me on TV, Mr. Fleshman. I have an urgent story that everyone needs to hear."

Officer Batterson faded into the woodwork as Fleshman guided her to the cameras. A fleeting moment of regret and worry nagged at her as she lifted the microphone. But she couldn't die without warning others that the Savannah Suicides weren't suicides at all, but a terrorist group spreading a deadly virus.

CRAIG AND THE DETECTIVES met back at the precinct to regroup, each second intense as they waited on news that the chopper or another patrol car had located Milaski.

"The local delivery service did not deliver the chocolates," Agent Black said. "They have no record of a delivery to the newspaper or Olivia Thornbird at all."

"Get Renard back in here," Craig ordered.

Black rushed to retrieve him from the holding cell. Then Craig stalked into the interrogation room and pounced on Renard as soon as he entered. "You're lying, Renard. Tell me where you got the virus."

Renard backed away, as if he might wet his pants. "I told you I don't know anything about the virus."

"We checked with that delivery service. They have no record of delivering anything to the paper that day."

Renard sank back in his chair, pale and shuddering. "I...swear I don't know. I would never do anything to hurt Olivia. And the guy who brought in the truffles was wearing a delivery service uniform."

Craig barely kept himself from choking Renard, but held back. His instincts told him the man was a scuzzball, but that he was telling the truth.

"He could have been in disguise," Black offered.

Craig motioned him to the hall, his mind ticking. "There was a story about several delivery service uniforms being sold on eBay a few weeks ago. See if you can track down the buyer."

Black nodded, but Detective Fox rushed up. "Olivia Thornbird's on TV, Horn. You'd better see this."

Shock bolted through Craig as they rushed to a nearby office where the set was already on. Fox was right. Olivia was sitting in front of a camera, a microphone in her hand. Her complexion appeared pasty, and…God, a red rash dotted her arms. She was getting worse. She needed to be hospitalized.

How much time did she have left? Would she be curable now?

"My name is Olivia Thornbird. I'm a reporter for the *Savannah Sentinel.* I'm not here to cause panic, but as a journalist, I believe the public has a right to know when they are in danger."

Craig cursed as she spilled the truth about her father's illness, the suspicion of a terrorist cell holding a dangerous virus, ready to unleash it on the public.

Why was she doing this? She'd promised him she'd wait. He'd agreed to give her the entire story, and last night…last night they'd made love, he'd thought they were working together.

He had to talk to her.

"There's going to be mass hysteria," Detective Black muttered.

"We need damage control," Fox snarled.

Craig's cell phone jangled, adding to the already anxious atmosphere. He hurriedly checked the ID log and grimaced at the sight of his father's number.

Not ready to deal with his political agenda, Craig ignored the call. "I'm going to the station," Craig said.

Black and Fox nodded. "I'll let you know if we get a lead on the delivery service uniforms or if we locate Milaski."

"Right." Craig headed outside to his car, jumped in and tore away from the station. When he got hold of Olivia, he was going to find out what the hell had happened to make her change her mind.

He'd thought that last night had meant something to her, as it had him.

Obviously he'd been a fool again. She'd used him as long as she could, even seduced him, and now spilled the story before they'd had a chance to find a cure for the virus or the person responsible for spreading it.

THE RASH HAD BEGUN to itch. Olivia felt feverish, dizzy, and her tongue was swelling inside her mouth. She hid her arms behind her back as the camera rolled to an end, then faced the shocked looks of the cameramen and newscasters. Their faces had turned chalky gray, making them blend into the bland stage background.

"Is that it? Do you have more?" Fleshman asked.

She shook her head, disoriented.

"Excuse me, Miss Thornbird." The receptionist who'd

greeted her earlier suddenly appeared. "There's a call for you. The man says it's important."

It might be Craig. Then again, she'd made a special plea for anyone who had any information about the virus or terrorist group to come forward, so this might be her lucky break. She followed the receptionist, well aware the director of the station and Officer Batterson dogged her to Fleshman's office.

But she refused to speak in front of them and insisted they stand outside the door while she answered the call.

"Hello, this is Miss Thornbird."

"Miss Thornbird, thank you for finally going public."

"What? Who is this?"

"If you want to know more about your father's death, then meet me."

She squeezed the phone with clammy fingers. "All right. Just tell me where."

"Serpent's Cove, Catcall Island side."

"I'll be there as soon as I can."

"You have something I've been looking for, don't you? A disk that contains some of your father's work."

She didn't have it, but she wasn't a fool. She wouldn't tell him that. "Yes, I have it."

"Then bring it with you."

She agreed, then hung up and checked over her shoulder. Officer Batterson was watching, and so was the director and Fleshman, so she positioned herself with her back to them so they couldn't see, then she shuffled through the desk until she found a blank disk. She grabbed it and stuck it in her purse, then turned and found Officer Batterson studying her with laser-like eyes, his angular jaw set tight.

"What's going on?" the director asked. "Was that news about the virus?"

Olivia shook her head. "No, I'm afraid it was personal, another story. But I'll let you know if I hear anything else."

He frowned, his brows knitted, but stepped aside. She strode toward the elevator, her heart pounding, her knees weak. She might be walking into a trap, but she had to prove that Craig was wrong about her father. He wasn't a traitor or a killer, but a hero who'd died studying the virus so he could save lives.

She only hoped she could stave off the effects of the virus until she could write the story.

"I need a lift," she said as Officer Batterson matched her stride.

His cool eyes skated over her. "Wherever you need to go, Miss Thornbird."

She hesitated. But she wasn't an idiot, wouldn't go without backup. "Okay, drive me to Serpent's Cove, but when we get there, stay a discreet distance away and cover me if I get in trouble. He warned me, no cops."

"Yes, ma'am." He opened the car door, and she slid inside.

He gave a clipped response, wrapped a dark hand around the steering wheel and pulled from the parking lot. The sights and sounds of Savannah faded as they drove, every minute ticking by a reminder that death waited to claim her. As they neared the island, Olivia regained her courage. "You can drop me anywhere along here," Olivia said. "I'll walk to the cove, just stay hidden in the woods."

He parked the car and turned toward her. In the shadows beneath the Spanish moss draping from the trees, his beady eyes glinted. Then he reached up and slowly peeled away the beard. Her breath caught in her throat as he revealed a small dark mole on his chin.

"Oh, my God. You're not Officer Batterson, are you?"

An icy sneer crossed his face just before he pointed a .45 at her chest.

Chapter Seventeen

Craig tried Olivia's cell phone on the way to the station, but she didn't answer. She was obviously avoiding him. He only hoped she was still there when he arrived. Part of him wanted to throttle her....

The other part ached to know that she was so ill.

How could he have trusted her, misread her so? And how could she betray him?

By the time he arrived at the TV station, the newscasters and staff were in an uproar, fending off panicked calls along with pranks and false leads that would have to be checked out. The director of the station met him up front, looking harried.

"Where's Olivia Thornbird?" Craig asked.

"She left about five minutes ago with that police officer."

"Where was she going?"

"She didn't say," the director replied with a judgmental glare. "I can't believe you guys kept this virus quiet."

Craig grimaced. "We were just trying to protect the investigation."

Two news anchors and a couple of their assistants

raced up. "The phones are ringing off the walls with worried citizens."

The director yanked at his tie. "And we've had a half dozen calls already with tips."

"I'll arrange for a police team to screen incoming calls for any possible leads," Craig said.

"Thanks." The director offered his hand. "We'll do everything we can to help, Agent Horn."

Craig nodded, punched in the number for Detective Black and made the arrangements. Agitation knotted the muscles at the base of his neck as he hung up. Separating the real calls from the phony ones was going to occupy valuable manpower and time, two things they were short on. He quickly turned back to the station director. "I need to find Miss Thornbird."

"Is she contagious?" one of the assistants asked.

Another anchorman tapped his heel in a nervous gesture. "Have we been exposed? Should we be tested?

The receptionist chewed a thumbnail. "Shouldn't she be in quarantine?"

"No, the virus is not contagious or airborne," Craig answered. "But it's imperative I find her. She's in danger."

"Miss Thornbird received a call before she left. My phone records all incoming calls," Fleshman said. "We could check it—"

"Let's go." Craig shot forward, not bothering for him to finish the sentence.

They rushed to Fleshman's office where he sorted through five more calls that had come in since, then played back the call to Olivia. Craig's pulse raced as he listened.

Five minutes later, he phoned Detective Black while he raced toward Serpent's Cove.

"I think she's meeting someone there, maybe even Milaski," Craig said.

"We got a lead on that delivery service uniform. Man named DJ Dunce bought several off of eBay." Black paused. "Bad news is that Dunce has a rap sheet a mile long. He's a hired assassin. And I checked with the vics' families—each one received a package containing food the week before they died."

At least that explained how the victims were infected.

"It's worse," Black said. "I tried Batterson but he didn't respond, so I sent a patrol car to Miss Thornbird's—"

"The station manager said Batterson was driving her—"

"No." Black cut him off. "That wasn't Batterson. Batterson's dead."

Oh, God. Pure panic suffused Craig. "Dunce has her. My guess is that he's taking her to meet Milaski."

And neither man would have any qualms about killing her.

If the virus didn't do it first.

OLIVIA SHUDDERED as the man she'd believed to be Officer Batterson yanked her from the car and pushed her forward across the sand. "You were the man in the hospital, the one who put me in the morgue?"

A wry laugh trilled in the breeze. The man's utterly calm manner chilled her to the bone. "You finally figured it out."

"But I don't understand. Who are you? Why have you been trying to kill me?"

"Just shut up and walk, lady."

She stumbled through the sea oats, dragging her feet in the grainy sand to slow herself down. He pressed the butt of the gun deeper into her back as he shoved her into a dark cave. The low-ceilinged interior felt dank, a shuffle of some kind of animal on the rocks making her skin crawl.

She wanted to scream, but the sound of the ocean roaring would drown out her cries if she did. Footsteps crunched on the ground below her. Then a tall, middle-aged bearded man in black appeared, the faint light spilling in through the cave illuminating his calculating eyes.

"We finally meet, Miss Thornbird."

The man with the gun shoved her to the ground, and she gripped the rough edges of the cave to steady herself as she searched for an escape. "Who are you?"

"Iska Milaski. I'm sure you've heard of me."

She gulped. "You have the virus. You're the one infecting people. But I don't understand why you're killing innocent people."

"Because your people killed mine," he said in a harsh voice. "Back in Egypt, your government used my people, some of my very own family, and infected them with this horrible disease."

Olivia shuddered. The United States had done that? "My father...my mother, they had nothing to do with that. I know they didn't."

His gaze slid over her. "I suppose you deserve to know the truth. It's too bad you won't live long enough to print it, though."

"Tell me," Olivia said. "Why did you infect my father?"

Milaski circled the cave, his quiet intensity as unnerving as the gun his hired killer held on her. "Your father was a nosy man. He refused to let your mother's death rest, but we had finally convinced him it wasn't safe for him to pursue the matter."

"My father wouldn't have backed down out of fear."

"Ah, you do not understand." His thick black brow rose sharply. "He was not afraid for himself, but for you."

The truth dawned on her. "You threatened to hurt me."

Milaski shrugged. "Was business."

"Did you kill my mother, too?"

"No," Milaski said. "I wanted her to keep working and save my people."

"I don't understand."

"Shubert was running the show then. He developed the germ strain that was tested in Egypt, but he sold it to a crazed scientist from the U.S. Instead of using their own subjects, though, they used our people. They wanted to win some stupid prize for their work." He spit out the words in disgust. "So for this prize, they made my mother, my father, my little brothers suffer."

"But my mother was trying to help save them."

"Yes. Unfortunately Shubert had her killed because she was going to expose him and the project."

Olivia pressed a shaky hand to her face where perspiration beaded and trickled down her cheek. This man wanted revenge for his people because they had suffered needlessly. She could understand that. But killing other innocents didn't make it right.

She swayed, a dizzy spell hitting her. Her head felt light, her words slurring as her tongue grew thicker. The rash was spreading, too. Now red dots covered her hands. "And when my father started working on this virus, he realized the similarities?"

"Exactly."

"But why wouldn't you want him to expose the people who'd hurt your family?"

Milaski shifted, the first sign of a conscience showing. "It was too late by then."

"I see. If my father made the connection back to the initial subjects used in Egypt, he might name you and stop you before you got your revenge." It all made sense in a twisted kind of way.

"We cannot go back now," Milaski said.

"The FBI is on to you," Olivia said. "They'll find you, stop you. You won't get away with it."

He gestured toward the hired gun, one hand indicating his patience was gone. "It is time."

Olivia balked, but Milaski shoved a small notepad and pen in her hand. "Now, Miss Thornbird, write your final story. Do it for my people and your own."

She shuddered. Instead of writing the story about the virus, he forced her to write a suicide note. Her hand trembled as she scribbled the words. Tears ached to push forward, but she blinked them back as she added a goodbye to Craig.

The page blurred, her head spun, and nausea rose to her throat. The ringing intensified in her head, and blood suddenly trickled from her nose. She shivered with fever, and the first tremor of a convulsion assaulted her.

Milaski's hired gun grabbed her arm, hauled her up and dragged her forward.

"It will be over soon, Miss Thornbird," Milaski said. "Death is much more peaceful than the virus effects. I'm certain your father welcomed it when it came, as did my family."

Anger hardened her resolve to live, but she stumbled and hit the dirt, tasted blood, then darkness swept her into unconsciousness. Seconds or minutes later, she didn't know which, Dunce yanked her up, hauled her from the cave through the knee-high sea oats. The heavy brush clawed at her arms as Dunce dragged her toward an overhang where the ocean roared below.

"Go ahead, Olivia," Dunce urged in a hypnotic monotone. "You can do it. Find peace in death as the others did."

The world blurred around her, a mixture of colors and emptiness. The voices in her head echoed as if bouncing through a canyon, their message urging her to throw herself off the cliff into the ocean, to let the tides take her to sea. Either that, or she could die a painful death beside this cold monster.

Her head throbbed, a cry catching in her throat as Craig's face materialized in her mind. Once he'd felt guilty for her father's death. Would he blame himself if she gave up now, too?

Dunce pushed the gun deeper into her lower back, his intent clear. Either she jumped or he would push her. Then again, maybe jumping would be the only way she might survive.

And maybe if she grabbed his arm, she could take the killer with her.

CRAIG WAS GOING out of his mind as he drove toward Serpent's Cove. He had no idea if the assassin had Olivia, or if Milaski did. Both were coldhearted killers.

"We traced Batterson's squad car to the cove," Detective Black said when Craig phoned for backup. "A team's on its way."

"I'll meet you there." Craig floored the engine and maneuvered around traffic through the narrow streets of Savannah, honking and yelling for people to get out of his way. The next ten minutes passed in a frenzy of heart-shattering images as he imagined what Olivia must be going through. Why hadn't she waited for him? Called him?

A truck swerved and nearly hit him; he slammed the horn again and cursed. Then he passed a Honda and raced over the bridge to Catcall Island. His pulse clamored as he neared Serpent's Cove and spotted the empty squad car.

Where was Olivia? Had they killed her and dumped her body in the ocean?

Sweat streaked his neck and back as he parked, jumped out and ran toward the cove. Several heart-pounding minutes later, he checked the cave and found it empty. A million scenarios raced through his head. All sickening.

Dear God, where was she?

He pivoted, scanned the area, the brush beyond. A big rock formation that resembled a hawk jutted out near the water's edge by an overhang that had sharp angles, reaching like talons toward the sea. His heart pounded. Then he glanced up and spotted Olivia.

She stood on the tip of the ledge, her hair flying in the wind, a streak of sunlight dappling golden rays that pitched her angelic face in murky lines. A tall, imposing man stood in the shadows behind her, a gun pressed to her back.

His own body lurched forward when she wobbled to the edge, her arms outstretched.

He shouted her name. "Olivia, no! Get back!"

His pulse racing, he ran through the sea oats to the steep, rocky path that led to the ledge and climbed the embankment. Rock and dirt skittered below his feet, pinging to the ground. Seagulls circled the shore. The waves crashed and broke with high tide, the noise drowning out his shouts as he ascended to the top.

His gun poised to fire, he climbed the last foot. Just as he crested the top, Olivia swayed as if she was disoriented. He saw blood on her cheek and perspiration on her forehead. Her symptoms were rapidly growing more acute. "Olivia?"

She didn't hear him. She grabbed the man's arm and wrestled with him, tried to pull him with her.

Then a gunshot rang out. He ducked to avoid it, and Olivia went soaring over the side of the cliff. Dunce leapt backward, running toward the woods. Craig yelled Olivia's name, ran for the ledge, saw her hit the water. Another gunshot pinged near his head, and he turned around, fury heating him as he unloaded shot after shot into Dunce's body. The man's face contorted, blood spurting from his chest as he sank to the ground.

Craig ran to the ledge. Had Olivia been shot?

He didn't have time to make it down the embankment. Without hesitation, he threw himself over the ledge and plunged into the crashing waves. Seconds later, he shoved up through the tide, searching for Olivia.

OLIVIA WAS FIGHTING the waves, struggling against the tide. She had to fight. Had to swim. Had to survive.

But the force of the tide caught her body, dragged her under again. She flapped her arms wildly, fought the wave, warned herself not to panic. But her injured shoulder throbbed, protested the brutal beating of the waves, and she was too weak to beat the strength of the undertow as it dragged her farther from land.

At last, she broke through the surface of the water. Gasped for a breath. Tried to shove the hair from her eyes. How far was she from the cove? Could she make it back?

No. The tides were sweeping her farther out to sea. The land…she could no longer see it. The cliff where she'd just been looked like a tiny pinpoint of light. A hurtling wave dragged her under again. She held her breath, let herself fall limp and tried to float with the current.

The voices in her head screamed at her to give up. She ordered herself to fight them as she broke to the surface again, coughing and sputtering. She thought she heard someone call her name. The sound echoed above the roar of the waves, drifted on the wind, then was carried out to sea.

She tried to swim toward the voice, clawed at the water, tasted the salt and sea, and choked. The salt stung her rash-stricken aching arms, and exhaustion stole her strength.

Through her feverish haze, she thought she heard her name again. But the wind and brutal water slapped her farther out, captured the sound and tossed it into the darkness. She was so weak, too. She couldn't fight it any longer.

She had her answers about her father now. About her mother. The truth.

And Craig…he didn't love her.

Then another vicious wave swept her into the sea, and she prayed for peace as the tides swallowed her.

CRAIG BROKE THROUGH the surface of the crashing waves, adrenaline surging through him as he spotted Olivia being swept under the water. He inhaled, then threw himself into motion, his arms gliding in even, rushed strokes as he swam toward her. The wind knocked him off pace, slowed him down, the undertow grabbing at his feet and sucking him into the vortex.

But he fought the panic and swelling riptide and raced through the waves, one stroke, two, another and another, until he was inches away from where he'd last seen her. "Olivia!"

She didn't answer. Hadn't surfaced…

He held his breath, then plunged below the surface again, searching frantically for her, swimming in a circle to see through the haze. A heartbeat later, he spotted her. Her blond hair floated around her in a wild frenzy, and her body was limp as she sank deeper toward the bottom of the ocean. He dove downward toward her, slid his arms around her waist and dragged her up to the surface. She gasped and choked as they broke through the wave.

"Damn it, hang on, Olivia. I need you."

A strangled sound erupted from her throat as she collapsed against him.

CRAIG HELD OLIVIA UNTIL the detectives and paramedics arrived, then reluctantly turned her over to the emergency room personnel when they reached the hospital. The EMTs had already started an IV and begun treating her for shock. They'd given her medication for the fever and were trying to make her comfortable.

The day and night bled into another. Hours stretched into eternity, hope dwindling with every agonizing second.

Detectives Black and Fox issued an APB on Milaski, calling for the FBI and NSA to issue a nationwide alert. Security checks at all airports, waterways and borders were put into effect. Detective Black phoned Dr. Carrington, who agreed to confer with Fulton along with another scientist from the CDC, about what was on the diskette.

Over twenty-four hours later, finally as the predawn sky broke with light, Craig clutched Olivia's hand and bowed his head, muttering a prayer for a miracle.

Dr. Carrington ducked his head in. "Agent Horn, Dr. Fulton's here. He says it's important."

Craig kissed Olivia's hand, then reluctantly left her and strode to the door. "What is it, Fulton?"

Fulton rubbed at his temple, a harrowed expression contorting his face. "I've studied the disk…should have come forward sooner. I was afraid I'd get in trouble, but I have to now."

"What's going on?" Craig snapped.

"I'm partially responsible for creating this virus, but I didn't know it at the time." He paused, as if it pained him to continue. "Last year, I was asked to study an old virus that was believed to have been used in Germany years ago. I created a mutated strain for biological warfare possibilities and later was contacted by Hal Oberman. He claimed he was working with a secret government organization that wanted the virus."

Craig snapped to alert. "Oberman, the head of the Department of Public Safety?"

"Yes, he said it was a classified government project to fight terrorism. At the time, I checked out the organization and it seemed legit. But when you came to see me, and after reviewing Thornbird's files and diskette, and after seeing Miss Thornbird on television earlier, I had to wonder."

"If your virus was the one attacking these people?" Craig asked.

Fulton pulled a hand down his face. "Yes. I...had no idea it was the same one, or that the organization wasn't doing what Oberman said. You have to believe me."

"You think Oberman sold the virus to Milaski?" Craig asked.

"I...I have no idea, but from the blood work I've studied, along with Thornbird's notes, it appears to be the same strain."

"I'll call Agent Devlin. Have him find Oberman." He gripped Fulton by the collar. "If you'd told us this sooner, we could have saved lives."

"I know," Fulton whimpered. "But I honestly believed Oberman was using it to fight terrorism. I didn't know that the organization might be bogus or that he might have other motives..."

As much as Craig hated to admit it, he could see how someone with authority might pull off a stunt like that. Information was often dispensed on a need-to-know basis. Security measures high, documents classified. A little tampering with the computer, or a bribe, and anything could be done.

Fulton's bony body shook beneath Craig's intense

gaze. "But listen. I think I might have an antidote for the virus."

The breath left Craig in a gush. "What?"

"After you showed up, I started looking back through Thornbird's notes and my own. I think there's a chance we can save Miss Thornbird."

Craig wanted to hope. But could he trust Fulton? "How do I know you're telling me the truth now?"

"I swear," Fulton said. "I'll go to jail afterward if you think I deserve it, but I'd like to at least try this antidote."

Craig glanced at Dr. Carrington. Olivia was dying. Growing weaker every minute. If they waited too long, there would be irreparable brain damage.

"All right. But Dr. Carrington will be monitoring you," Craig said. After all, if there was any chance of saving Olivia, they had to take it.

Chapter Eighteen

Olivia drifted in and out of oblivion. First, the pain had been too much, and she'd welcomed the darkness. But Craig's husky voice had beckoned her back.

"Please, Olivia, it's been two days. I need you. Don't leave me."

She had been the one to beg him not to leave her earlier. Before they'd made love. Then he'd betrayed her.

"Olivia, I don't know why you didn't call me before you went to the station, but I don't care. We can work it out, just stay with me, sweetheart."

Sweetheart? No man had ever called her a pet name. She had to straighten Craig out. She wasn't sweet or needy or any of those female things; she was Olivia Thornbird. She stood up for what she thought was right. For what she wanted.

And she wanted to live. To come back to Craig.

But he would hate her for going public.

And she couldn't let him decimate her father's name; he'd died to protect her.

She wiggled her fingers and tried to open her eyes, but she felt so groggy it took considerable effort, and three tries. Finally, she looked into his somber gray eyes. Eyes that had once been icy and emotionless now held pain and worry. And some other emotion she couldn't quite put her finger on.

"Olivia?"

"Yes," her voice rasped, low, a mere whisper.

"You're going to be all right. Dr. Fulton created an antidote from your father's research." He squeezed her hand between his own, and she was grateful for the warmth.

"I'm sorry…" Her voice broke. "I went on TV. I thought you'd used me, that it was the right thing to do to help the people…"

Her throat was so dry that her voice trailed off into a cough. He lifted a cup of water and slid a straw to her lips, and she drank greedily. "I heard the phone message from your father, that you thought my dad created the virus, that he killed those people. And you had files on me…"

His eyes darkened with emotions. "I was just doing my job, Olivia. I didn't want to believe your father was guilty. Hell, even when I suspected him, I refrained from telling you because I didn't want to hurt you."

Her chest ached. "I…I'm sorry about the TV airing—"

"Shh." He pressed a finger to her lip. "You were right this time. When Fulton saw your plea, he came forward, confessed that he gave the virus to Oberman, the director of the DPS. Devlin phoned. Oberman's in custody now."

"What…what about Milaski and the virus?"

"I spoke with Agent Devlin about an hour ago. Milaski's chopper went down. He died in the crash, and the virus went up in flames with him."

"The…man who tried to kill me?"

The image of the man pushing the gun into her back played through her head, making her grip the sheet tighter.

He tensed, as if he were reliving the image himself. "He was a hired assassin—he's dead, too. We still don't know who trained him though, but we'll look into it."

Olivia tried to sit up, but he gently coaxed her to lie back down. "You have to rest, Olivia."

"I'm fine now. You can go."

Craig frowned. "But…"

"The case is over, Craig. You thought my father was guilty, you kept things from me. I can't forget that." She licked her lips for courage. "Besides, we'll always look at things differently."

Ignoring the crushed look in his eyes, she rolled to her side, shutting him out. She might be okay now, but she had no idea what long-term side effects she might suffer from the virus. She couldn't take the chance of becoming ill later or an invalid. She absolutely wouldn't ask Craig to take care of her.

The sound of Craig's footsteps clattering against the floor felt like knives in her chest. Then the door closed behind him, and she covered her eyes. Tears slid through her fingertips and dropped onto the pillowcase.

She loved Craig desperately, but she'd never allow herself to need anyone again, to be left alone as she had been when her mother and father had died.

CRAIG'S HEART CLENCHED at Olivia's dismissal. He'd thought if she survived they might work things out. That she'd confess her love. But she'd just bid him goodbye.

He sank onto the cold vinyl sofa in the waiting room to compose himself, willing his emotions in check. It was better this way. He didn't need a woman messing with his mind. He could go back to being the Iceman.

But, damn it, he loved her.

And even if he wanted the Iceman back, he might be gone forever.

Agent Devlin, coffee in hand, stepped up to him. "She's going to make it?"

He nodded. "Did you question Oberman?"

"He claims he didn't sell the virus to Milaski, that someone on his staff did. When Oberman found out, he did everything he could to find out the source. He's named names, and we have a guy named Denasky in custody."

Not for the first time, Craig wondered about his own father's involvement. But hadn't he done the same thing to a degree—tried to keep the investigation quiet to protect citizens from panic? He supposed he, Oberman and his father were more alike than he wanted to admit.

"You told Olivia the virus has been destroyed?"

He balled his hands into fists. "Yes."

"Then why the long face?"

Craig winced.

"You know, Horn," Devlin said in a deep voice. "If you love her, you should hold on to her."

He jerked his head up. The two men had never discussed their personal lives.

"I made a mistake once, lost the woman of my dreams." Devlin grimaced. "Sometimes I'm not sure the job is worth it."

He was right. Craig couldn't give up his job, and he'd

never ask Olivia to, but they could have a relationship if they tried hard enough.

That is, if she loved him.

Just as he stood, debating what to do, his father raced into the waiting room. "I came as soon as I heard you took Hal Oberman into custody."

Jeez, did his father never quit? "Listen, Dad, we had to." He explained the circumstances. "Oberman should have come to us sooner. His hush operation cost people their lives."

"He was trying to protect the public—"

"He was trying to protect himself, just like you always do. Just like you did when my sister died."

His father's expression hardened. "That was different. I was trying to protect you and your mother. There are things you don't know."

Craig glared at him. "Because you chose to keep them quiet."

"Don't tell me you don't do the same thing, Craig. You make deals with known criminals, put them into witness protection programs all the time." He pinned him with an angry look. "And until you got involved with that reporter, you managed to keep this virus out of the news."

Craig grimaced. "Olivia Thornbird survived, and as I promised her, she'll write the story."

His father ran a manicured hand over his chin. "But you have to stop her. Her news report earlier was inexcusable."

Craig had detested his father the day he'd covered up his sister's death. He almost hated him more now. "Olivia has a mind of her own, Dad. She's intelligent, a responsible journalist, and she almost died because too many people wanted to keep things quiet."

"But she was just using you," his father said. "Don't you see that?"

Remembering Olivia's dismissal a few moments earlier, Craig momentarily wavered. But his father was wrong.

"Use her the same way she used you," his father said. "Go in there and persuade her to kill the story, or at least soften it."

Craig squared his shoulders, no longer caring what his father thought. "The only thing I intend to do with Olivia is convince her to marry me."

Emboldened by the memory of the way she'd given herself to him that night, the way he'd felt when they made love, he pivoted and strode toward Olivia's room. She hadn't just been using him…not Olivia.

Besides, normally he didn't give up so easily when he wanted something. And he wanted Olivia.

Inhaling to calm his raging nerves, he pushed open the door and walked inside.

"Olivia?"

Olivia's vibrant blue eyes met his, but they were red-rimmed as if she'd been crying. "I…thought you'd left."

"No."

He stalked toward her, then stopped beside her bed, his heart pounding. "What in the hell's going on?" he asked in a gruff whisper. "I thought we had something special the night we made love."

"Craig, please…"

"You blame me for your father's death?"

"No."

"You hate the fact that I'm with the FBI?"

She shook her head. "I admire your work, you should know that. I...thought you hated reporters."

His frown slackened slightly. "I used to, but you've, uh, grown on me."

A small smile flickered in her eyes, offering him hope, so he threw himself out on the front line, feeling as exposed as if he were standing and fighting in enemy territory.

"Listen, Olivia, I love you. Tell me you don't love me, and I'll walk out of here and never come back."

Her lower lip quivered. "I...can't."

His heart shattered. "You can't say you love me, or you can't deny it?"

"What if there are side effects to this virus, long-term ones like Shubert suffered?" she said in an anguished whisper. "I don't want, no, I *won't,* be a burden to any man."

Realization dawned. The independent Olivia was back. Afraid of losing herself. Of being hurt. He saw the tough exterior now, but knew the sweet tenderness below that hard surface, the sultry passionate woman that belonged to him. "You could never be a burden, Olivia."

"But we both saw Shubert..."

"That's not going to happen to you," he murmured. "You're cured."

"But what if later on—"

"Olivia, listen to me." He cupped her face between his hands. "You and I both know there's no assurance of tomorrow. I work a dangerous job, and...you do, too. But one thing I've learned from this virus, from almost losing you, is that we have to live for today." He paused, his throat thick. "I don't want to be alone. Not anymore."

She clutched the sheets between her fingers. "I want to believe we can work it out, Craig, but our jobs…we might be in conflict again."

"I thought we made a pretty good team. We both have integrity, respect for each other. We'll work it out."

"You really think so?"

"Yes, neither one of us has to live in a vacuum, not when we love each other." He hesitated, his heart picking up its pace. "You do love me, don't you?"

Tears filled her eyes. "Yes… I do. I love you, Craig."

He pressed a kiss to her lips. "And I love you. I want you as my lover, my friend, my wife." He brushed her hair back gently. "Marry me, Olivia."

A sultry smile tilted her mouth as she looped her arms around his neck. "Yes, Craig, I'll marry you."

He framed her face, then kissed her again, this time with all the passion and pent-up fear that he'd struggled with the past two nights, when he'd thought he might lose her forever.

The buried secrets were no longer buried, but unearthed, unable to hold either of them back. Nothing mattered except that they'd found each other.

"Look, it's going to be a beautiful day," he whispered as the sun streaked through the window. "And we're going to spend the rest of them together, Olivia."

She pressed a finger to his lip and hugged him to her. "Yes, as husband and wife."

Epilogue

Craig straightened his tie, his hands shaking slightly. Today was his wedding day.

A day he'd thought would never come.

Since his engagement, his co-workers at the agency had teased him mercilessly—he'd lost his legendary title of being the Iceman.

A loss he could deal with, as long as he had Olivia by his side.

He moved toward the door, ready to take his place in the white gazebo Olivia had rented for their wedding. It would be a small affair overlooking the ocean, where the bright sunshine warmed them with promises of better days, of endless tomorrows and passionate heated nights.

To his surprise, the door squeaked open and his father appeared, dressed in a gray suit, his expression serious. Craig hadn't spoken to him since the day he'd come to the hospital, and he hadn't invited him to the wedding.

He hoped to hell there wasn't trouble or a nationwide emergency to darken his wedding day or drag him away. Then again, maybe his father had come to try to talk him out of marrying Olivia.

"Son."

"Dad, I wasn't expecting you."

"You know your mother would be crushed if she missed your wedding day."

He stared at his father, unwilling to deny the distance between them.

"And—" his father cleared his throat "—I wanted to be here, too."

Craig narrowed his eyes. "Dad, if you're trying to persuade me not to marry Olivia, it won't work—"

His father held up his hand. "That's not why I'm here. In fact, I read her story on the virus. It was…" He paused and cleared his throat again. "Very well done."

Craig couldn't contain a smile. "She is talented."

"Yes. And tenacious," his father said.

He still had no idea where his father was going, but he chuckled. "Yes, that, too."

"I…I think she might be an asset to this family."

God, no, his father wasn't still on that bandwagon. "You won't compromise her values, Dad—"

"No, I didn't mean it like that." His father turned sheepish. "I meant I like her spunk, her ability to tell the truth without sensationalizing things. She did an excellent job reminding people of the balance between the press reporting the truth and supposition. And of the hard choices the police and people have to make."

Craig nodded.

"And of convincing me to come today."

Craig's hand flexed on his tie. "Olivia invited you?"

He nodded. "Yes. We, uh, she thought we should straighten something out." His dad ran a hand through his neatly combed hair. "You accused me of covering up your sister's death for my own political gain. I admit that a scandal wouldn't have helped me in my campaign, but that's not the real reason I did it."

"What other reason could there be?"

"I wanted to protect you and your mother. You were so young, I didn't want you to know. But now…now you're grown up. You have a right."

He'd never seen his father stumbling for words before. "Dad, what are you trying to tell me?"

"Son…your sister was a p—" he cleared his throat, then spit out the word "—prostitute." His face paled as he produced a brown envelope. He opened it with jerky movements, then let the pictures fall from the inside onto the table. The photographs told the story. "At sixteen, she ran with a bad crowd, got involved in doing porn flicks. I had no idea…and neither did your mom." His voice broke. "I think she did it to get back at us, to hurt us. And by the time I found out, she was hooked on heroin. Too far gone to reach." He paused, squeezed the bridge of his nose. "Believe me, I tried. I dragged her kicking and screaming to rehab twice…."

Craig winced.

"You were fourteen, an adolescent struggling in high school. I thought…it would be bad for you if the truth got out."

Craig's hands felt clammy as he dragged them from the pictures. His father was right. The kids at school— it would have been hard. Awful.

The truth hit him. His father had buried their family secrets to protect him.

"Mom…"

"Still doesn't know. She honestly believes your sister died in a car accident."

Craig imagined his mother's reaction—the hurt, the pain, the guilt she would feel—if she knew the truth.

Wouldn't he have done the same thing as his father if it meant sparing someone he loved the agony of such a horrible truth?

He stuffed the photos back in the envelope, willing the gruesome images at bay. What a terrible burden for his father to have to bear all alone.

And how he'd misjudged him.

He reached out his hand, shook his father's, then choked as his dad pulled him into his arms.

"I'm so proud of you, son." His father's voice warbled. "I know I haven't acted like it or told you, but I am."

"Thank you, Dad." Craig's own throat felt thick. "Would you be my best man?"

His father nodded, his eyes moist. Then the door squeaked open, and Craig's mother poked her head in. "Come on, you guys. 'The Wedding March' is about to begin! Olivia will leave if you don't get up there soon."

OLIVIA'S FINGERS TRAILED lovingly over the lace of her mother's wedding gown. She'd found the scooped-neck silk and taffeta design in the attic, and had it cleaned for the day. A smile filled her heart as she fingered the beautiful strand of pearls around her neck, then her gaze drifted to the pearl earrings that glistened in the light. Somehow, wearing her mother's things made her feel close to her again, as if she were standing right beside her.

She gripped the bouquet of roses in her hand, smiling at the sight of Craig standing beneath the gazebo in back of his cabin by the seashore, his father by his side. Apparently the two men had made up.

Her smile grew wider.

She'd had her work cut out talking to the senator. But she'd insisted that family was important, and that if she and Craig had children, she wanted them to know their grandparents.

The idea of grandchildren had seemed to turn things around.

"The Wedding March" began, and she slowly walked across the grass, the lacy train trailing her on the soft grass as the ocean waves crashed and broke on the shore. An image of her parents came to her, and she hugged it to herself, knowing that they were with her in spirit.

Then she looked up and saw Craig's smile, saw the heat and hunger flare in his eyes, and her body erupted into fire.

The ceremony was simple, fast, but their vows were heartfelt. And the secrets that had been buried were no longer there to stand between them.

As Craig slid the simple gold band on her finger, he whispered his love and she whispered hers in return. Then he took her in his arms and kissed her, and she knew that their marriage would last a lifetime.

* * * * *

Look for Rita Herron's upcoming novella,
"An Angel for Christmas,"
part of the EPIPHANY anthology
in November 2005,
when she joins forces with
Debra Webb and Mallory Kane
for a suspenseful holiday treat,
only in Harlequin Intrigue.

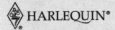
HARLEQUIN®

INTRIGUE®

and

JOANNA WAYNE

present

SECURITY MEASURES

September 2005

Falsely imprisoned, Vincent Magilenti had
broken out of jail to find Candy Owens,
the mother of his child and the woman
whose testimony had sent him away.
But when their daughter disappeared,
Vincent would do whatever it took to
protect them…even if it meant going
back to prison.

*Available at your
favorite retail outlet.*

eHARLEQUIN.com

The Ultimate Destination for Women's Fiction

For **FREE online reading,** visit
www.eHarlequin.com now and enjoy:

Online Reads
Read **Daily** and **Weekly** chapters from
our Internet-exclusive stories by your
favorite authors.

Interactive Novels
Cast your vote to help decide how these
stories unfold...then stay tuned!

Quick Reads
For shorter romantic reads, try our
collection of Poems, Toasts, & More!

Online Read Library
Miss one of our online reads?
Come here to catch up!

Reading Groups
Discuss, share and rave with other
community members!

For great reading online,
visit www.eHarlequin.com today!

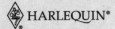